'But...would you feel honourable about violating my person? A woman who's never been kissed?'

His eyes flickered over her face and throat. She could sense his hesitation, his struggle against temptation. It gave her such an exhilarating feeling to see that she could tempt him from his intent. And he *would* succumb, she realised with a thrilled, almost incredulous certainty, her heart thundering.

Beneath his black lashes his pupils flared like a hungry wolf's.

He curled his lean fingers under her jaw. 'That can be fixed,' he said. Then he brought his lips down on hers with deliberate, sensual purpose.

At that first firm touch, a fiery tingling sensation shot through her veins like an electric charge, and sent an immediate swell of warmth to her breasts. She tried to remember he was her adversary, and made a half-hearted attempt to cool her response, but he drew her in closer. Then, like the cunning devil he was, he softened the kiss to clever, gentle persuasion, until the fire on her lips ignited her bloodstream and aroused all her secret, intimate places with erotic yearning.

UNTAMED BILLIONAIRE, UNDRESSED VIRGIN

BY
ANNA CLEARY

First published in Great Britain 2008
This edition published 2010
Harlequin Mills & Boon Limited,
Eton House, 18-24 Paradise Road, Richmond, Surrey TW9 1SR

© Anna Cleary 2008

ISBN: 978 0 263 21024 8

Harlequin Mills & Boon policy is to use papers that are natural, renewable and recyclable products and made from wood grown in sustainable forests. The logging and manufacturing process conform to the legal environmental regulations of the country of origin.

Printed and bound in Great Britain
by CPI Antony Rowe, Chippenham, Wiltshire

As a child, **Anna Cleary** loved reading so much that during the midnight hours she was forced to read with a torch under the bedcovers, to lull the suspicions of her sleep-obsessed parents. From an early age she dreamed of writing her own books. She saw herself in a stone cottage by the sea, wearing a velvet smoking jacket and sipping sherry, like Somerset Maugham.

In real life she became a schoolteacher, where her greatest pleasure was teaching children to write beautiful stories.

A little while ago, she and one of her friends made a pact to each write the first chapter of a romance novel in their holidays. From writing her very first line Anna was hooked, and she gave up teaching to become a full-time writer. She now lives in Queensland, with a deeply sensitive and intelligent cat. She prefers champagne to sherry, and loves music, books, four-legged people, trees, movies and restaurants.

For Gabi, Ben, Michelle, Jenny, Mirandi, Tina, Vicki, Terese and Shirley, with love and appreciation.

CHAPTER ONE

CONNOR O'BRIEN'S plane glided into Sydney on the first rays of dawn. The shadowy city materialised below, a mysterious patchwork of rooftops and dark sea, emerging from the mists of night. The comforts it promised were welcome, after the deserts he'd traversed over the last five years in the dubious name of Intelligence, but Connor expected no feeling of homecoming. To him Sydney was just another city. Its spires and skyscrapers felt no more connected to him than the mosques and minarets he'd left behind.

Once on the ground, he breezed through customs, courtesy of his diplomatic status. His honed blending-in skills spared him any undue attention. He was just another tall Australian in the Foreign Service.

The technicalities taken care of, he strolled across the International Terminal with his long easy stride, his single suitcase in tow, laptop case in his spare hand. From force of habit, with covert skill he scanned the groups of sleepy relatives waiting to embrace their loved ones. Wives and girlfriends beaming up at their men and weeping, children running into their fathers' arms. For him, no one. With his father gone now, he kept no personal connections. No lives at risk for knowing him. His precious anonymity was intact. Not a soul to know or care if Connor O'Brien lived or died, and that was how it had to be.

The glass exit doors opened before him and he walked out into the Australian summer dawn, safe and secure in his solitariness. The sky had lightened to a pale grey, washing out the street lamps to a wan hue. Even for the height of midsummer the morning was warm. The faintest whiff of eucalyptus wafted to him on the breeze like the scent of freedom.

Scanning for the taxi rank, he felt an unaccustomed buzz.

He rubbed his bristly jaw and contemplated the potential amenities of a good hotel. Shower, breakfast, relax with the newspapers, shake off the jet lag…

'Mr O'Brien?'

A uniformed chauffeur stepped forward from the open rear door of a limo parked in line with the exit. Respectfully he touched his cap. 'Your lift, sir.'

Connor stilled, every one of his nerves and trigger-sharp reflexes on instant alert.

A thin, querulous voice issued from inside the car. 'Come on, come on, O'Brien. Give Parkins your gear and let's get on the road.'

Connor knew that voice. With disbelief he peered into the dim interior. A small elderly man swam into focus, majestically ensconced in the plush upholstery.

Sir Frank Fraser. Wily old fox, *legend* of the Service and one of his father's old golfing cronies. But surely the ex-Chief had long since hung up his cloak and dagger and retired to live on the Fraser family fortune? As far as Connor knew, he was now a respectable pillar of the world of wealth and ease.

'Well, what are we waiting for?' The quavery voice held the autocrat's note of incredulity at not being instantly obeyed.

Curiosity outweighed Connor's chagrin at having his moment of freedom curtailed, so he handed his suitcase to the hovering Parkins and slid into the old guy's travelling suite.

At once his smooth, bronzed hand was seized in a wrinkled claw and shaken with vigour.

'Good to see you, O'Brien.' The ancient autocrat took in

Connor's long limbs, his lean, athletic frame, with an admiring gaze. 'And, my God, you're the living image of your old man. Same colouring, Mick's build—everything.'

Connor didn't try to deny it. Sure, like his father, he'd inherited the ink-black hair, dark eyes and olive skin of some tall, long ago Spaniard who'd washed up on the Irish coast from the storm-scattered Armada, but his father had been a family man, and there the resemblance had to end.

'And you've done well. What department has the embassy hired you for? Humanitarian Affairs, isn't it?'

'Something like that,' Connor allowed as the limo started and nosed into the road for the city. He smiled. 'Humanitarian Advisor to the First Secretary for Immigration.'

Sir Frank's aged face settled into thoughtful lines. 'Yes, yes, I can see why they need more lawyers. There'd be plenty of work involved there.'

A vision of the horror he'd had to deal with at the Australian Embassy in Baghdad swam into Connor's mind. Unable even to begin describing it, he merely shrugged acknowledgement, waiting for his father's old mate to spill what was on his mind.

Sir Frank sent him a glance that penetrated through to the back of his brain, and said with unnerving perspicacity, 'Isn't all that tragedy enough to keep you interested, without this other work you're doing? Your father always told me the law was your first and only love.'

Connor controlled every muscle not to react, though a little nerve jumped somewhere in his gut. 'Sir Frank, is there something behind this friendly chat? Something you need to tell me?'

Sir Frank drew a cigar from his breast pocket. 'Let's just say we have a friend of a friend in common.'

Connor's ears pricked up. This was agency speak for *contact*. So why the old lion and not some field operative? He was considering the possibilities when Sir Frank came in with a low hit.

'Heard about your losing your wife and child. That was tough. There's too many of these planes going down. How long ago was it now?'

Connor gripped his case while the dust and ashes settled back in his soul. The force of it could still catch him off guard, even now. 'Nearly six years. But—'

The elderly voice softened a notch. 'Must be time you tried again, lad. A man needs a woman, kids to come home to. It's time you stopped all this adventuring and settled down. Take up the threads again. This sort of work in Baghdad…' He shook his head. 'A man burns out fast. Two or three years should be the limit, and you're well past it. I hear you've taken some very close shaves. They tell me you're good—the very best—but a man only stays on top of the game for so long.' He slid Connor a glance. 'The man you replaced ended up with a knife through his gullet.'

Connor gazed at him with a mixture of incredulity and sardonic amusement. 'Thanks.'

But the old guy was in earnest. As his enthusiasm heated up his gnarled hands gesticulated with increasing fervour. 'I wouldn't be doing my duty to Mick if I didn't say this, young fella. You're dicing with death.'

'You should know,' Connor fired back. 'You diced with it yourself long enough.'

'That's right, I did, and I've learned what's important. No one ever wins this game.' He grasped Connor's arm. 'Look, I could pull a few strings for you. Your dad's left you a wealthy man. You could set up your own firm. There's always a call for good lawyers in this country.' He thumped his creaky old knee with his thumb. 'Plenty of injustice *right here*. A big handsome lad like you won't take long to find another lovely girl.'

The permafrost that passed for Connor's heart since the real thing had been broken and scattered over a Syrian mountainside registered nothing. He knew what he'd lost and would never have again. He made his way now without attachments. Banter, the occasional dalliance with a pretty woman, were sufficient to keep the shadows at bay.

'Civilian life offers its challenges, too,' Sir Frank persisted. '*And* its excitements.' He waved his unlit cigar. 'What are you now—thirty? Thirty-five?'

'Thirty-four.' In spite of his discipline Connor felt his abdominal muscles clench. He understood well enough what the old guy was alluding to. To perform in Intelligence an officer needed to be as clinical and objective towards his contacts as a machine. Perhaps, for some, cracks could develop over time and emotion begin to leak in, but *he* had no need to be concerned. He was still as balanced and dispassionate in his work as ever. He'd quit soon enough if he had a reason. In fact, he needed the constant threat of death to realise he was alive.

'Sir Frank,' he said in his deep, quiet voice, 'your concern is appreciated, but unnecessary. If there's something you need to tell me, spit it out. Otherwise your driver can drop me right here.'

Sir Frank looked approvingly at him. 'A straightshooter, just like Mick. Exactly like him.' He shook his head and sighed. 'If only Elliott could straighten himself out.'

Ah. At last. The crunch.

Connor stared broodingly out at the familiar streets, riffling back through the dusty mental files of family connections. 'Isn't Elliott your son?'

'Now *that's* what I wanted to talk to you about. A situation has arisen.'

As far as he knew, Elliott Fraser was one of those wealthy, fifty-ish CEOs in the private sector. 'He's involved in something?'

The old man looked gloomy. 'You might say *something*. A woman.'

Connor drew an austere breath. 'Look, I think you may have been misinformed, Sir Frank. I'm here on leave.' His tone was cool, but it was necessary to let the old guy feel the steel edge of his refusal. 'I haven't been flown halfway around the world to sort out your son's love-life.'

Sir Frank's indignant weedy frame flared up like a firecracker. 'That's exactly what you have been flown here for, *mister*,' he retorted with spirit. 'Who do you think got you your leave?' He gestured vehemently with his cigar, pointing it in Connor's face. 'No need to get cocky with me, fella, just because I knew you when you had your milk teeth. That's the very reason I've chosen *you*.'

Before Connor could respond, Sir Frank leaned forward and pinned him with an urgent, beady gaze. 'It won't interrupt your break much, Connor. It'll take you a week, a fortnight at most, then you can enjoy the rest of your three months. Who knows? You might decide to stay longer. Anyway, I know you'll do your best to help me out. For the love of Mick.'

Ah, here it was. The old boys' friendship card. All those mornings out on the green. Boozy afternoon sessions in the clubhouse. Connor knew it for what it was—emotional blackmail, and impossible to reject. He closed his eyes for an instant, then resigned himself.

'All right, all right. Go on, then. Shoot.'

'That's better.' Sir Frank sat back, satisfaction momentarily deepening the cracks and crevices in his crocodile-skin face. 'Now, this is strictly between us. Elliott's being considered for a top job with the ministry. Very hush-hush. He can't afford any scandal. Not a whiff.' He held up a wizened hand. 'No, it's serious. Marla is in America on business for her firm. If she comes back and finds out he's been playing away from home…' He shuddered. 'Marla can be very forceful. I have a strong instinct about this, Connor, and my instincts are rarely wrong. The chances are that this little popsy he's got himself entangled with is a plant. The timing is suspicious. But even if she *isn't*…' He closed his wrinkled eyelids in deprecation. 'Do you see now why I've chosen you? I don't want the agency involved. This is my *family*…I can't risk some stranger.' He moved closer to Connor and lowered his voice. 'You'll be on your own entirely. It has to be strictly between you and me.' He waggled an admonitory finger. 'No logging into the agency's tech services.'

Connor shook his head in bemusement. 'But surely all you have to do is whisper in Elliott's ear?'

'You try doing that with Elliott. He thinks he's keeping her under wraps.'

Connor concealed his amusement. The old guy was clearly loath to reveal to his son that he was keeping tabs on him.

Sir Frank clutched at his wrist. 'Connor, for all his sins, Elliott's my *son*. And then there's my grandson.' His rheumy old eyes filled up with tears. 'He's four years old.'

Connor noticed a tremor in the frail, liver-spotted hand grasping his sleeve and felt the faintest twinge in his chest. 'Right,' he said, exhaling a long breath. Old people and children had always been his Achilles' heel. He might as well grit his teeth, agree to the task and get it over with. He straightened his wide shoulders, and, needing to rein in the excess of emotion lapping the walls of the limo, injected some professional briskness into his voice. 'Do you have anything on the woman?'

Sir Frank conquered his tears with amazing swiftness and switched into business mode. Reaching into an alcove set in the door, he produced a file. 'Her name's Sophy something. Woodford…no… Wood*ruff*. Works in the Alexandra.'

'Where's that?' Connor said, flipping the single page. The information was sparse. A few dates and times. Meetings with Elliott in coffee shops. A bar. An indistinct CCTV still of a slim, dark-haired woman. Her face wasn't quite in focus, but the camera had managed to catch something of the delicacy of an oval face, the lustre of longish, wavy dark hair. Employed as a speech pathologist in a paediatric clinic. A good, conservative cover. Like his own.

'You know Macquarie Street?'

'Who doesn't?' As the avenue in which both the Botanical Gardens and the Opera House resided, Macquarie Street was one of the finest boulevards in Sydney. It had long been the preserve of the high-fliers of the medical profession.

'Some rooms have been vacated for you there. Your law practice will be a perfect cover.' The old tycoon added slyly, 'If you did decide to stay, there'd be nothing to stop you hanging up your shingle there for real.'

The location was just around the corner from some of the wealthiest bastions of the legal profession. Connor supposed he could get away with setting up as a lawyer in doctors' territory. Just how dangerous did the old guy expect the assignment to be? He felt some misgivings at the amorphous nature of it. Sir Frank's reputation as a cunning operator was well earned.

He studied the clever old face. 'What exactly do you want from me?'

'Find out about her. Her background, connections, everything. She's almost certainly working for a foreign state. *Pillow* talk.' He shook his head in disgust. 'You'd think Elliott would have enough savvy to…' He broke off, ruminating on his son's naiveté with compressed lips. 'Anyway, if—*if*—you find she's just a little gold-digger looking for a lamb to fleece, pay her off.'

Connor winced. From what he'd heard of Elliott Fraser, his lamb-like qualities were highly doubtful. On the surface, though, it seemed a tame little assignment. Nothing like strolling to an evening rendezvous to meet a contact dressed in high explosives. Hardly in the same universe as drinking coffee with a smiling man who was preparing to slice open his throat.

'A good-looking lad like you won't have any trouble getting close to the woman.'

Connor flashed him a wry glance. He didn't do *close*. He was just about to set him straight on that issue when the limo turned into a tree-lined avenue, and he recognised the graceful colonial architecture of Macquarie Street.

Traffic was minimal at this early hour, and there was time to appreciate the street's pleasantness, enhanced on one side by the dense green mystery of the Botanical Gardens burgeoning with summer growth behind a long stretch of tall, iron railings.

Halfway along the street the chauffeur pulled into the kerb.

'The Alexandra,' Sir Frank announced.

Connor craned to stare up at a honey-coloured sandstone edifice, several storeys in height. A splash of scarlet flowers spilled from a third-floor window ledge.

'You'll find your rooms on the top floor. Suite 3E.' Sir Frank pressed a set of old-fashioned keys into Connor's hand. 'Mind you keep in touch with me every step of the way.' He sat back and pulled on his blank cigar, then added excitedly, 'You know, Connor, I have a very good feeling about this now. I'm sure you'll be just the man to stop clever little Miss Sophy Woodruff in her tracks.'

CHAPTER TWO

SHADOW. Just a touch to enhance the blue of her irises. Violet like her name, her father used to say. Her official name, not that she'd ever use it. Thank goodness it only rarely appeared, usually on government documents or bank statements. What sort of people would call their child something so schmaltzy?

Certainly not the parents she knew. They'd felt obliged to keep it, but everyone had preferred to call her by the name they'd chosen themselves. Sophy was her father's choice. Henry—her *real* father, not the biological one.

That uncomfortable feeling coiled in her stomach. Her biological father. Such a cold descriptor. But could he really be as cold as he seemed? How warm was any man likely to feel when he encountered the daughter he never knew he had? Or so he'd said. Still, if he'd been lying, why order the DNA test?

He was lying about something, though, she could feel it in her bones.

Her brows were dark enough, closer to black than her hair. One quick pencil stroke to define their natural arch. In an emergency it would have to do.

Mascara was mandatory. Lashes could never be too long or too thick. A quick brush of blush on her cheekbones to warm the pallor of her broken night's sleep, but a glance at the clock decided her to be satisfied with that if she wanted to catch the 6.03 ferry.

With the heatwave still roasting Sydney after three days, she needed to wear something cool. She slipped on a straight, knee-length skirt, turned sideways to check in the mirror. Flat enough. Her lilac shirt with its pretty cap-sleeves was fresh from the cleaners' and required no ironing. She snatched up her handbag and slid into her lucky high heels.

Something told her there'd be running ahead. Tuesdays were seldom her best, but she had a very strong feeling about this one. She was on the verge of something, she could tell by the prickling in the back of her neck.

Zoe and Leah, her housemates, were barely stirring. She battled her way around the pile of camping gear they'd assembled in the hall, flung them a hasty 'Bye,' and ran down the path to the gate, the sun barely up. For the thousandth time she retraced in her mind every step she'd taken since she'd picked the registered letter up from the post office in yesterday's lunch hour.

She'd taken it straight back to her office to read. And there it had been. Official confirmation. Elliott Fraser's DNA profile matched sufficiently with hers for the lab to attest that he was her father.

She'd placed it in her bag, and felt sure she still had it when she went to help Millie, in the office next door, pack up for her move.

It hadn't been until she arrived home that she'd realised it was missing. After the initial panic, she remembered pausing in the mothers' room on the way from the Ladies. That had to be right…Sonia from the ophthalmic clinic had been in there having a weep, and she'd dragged out a handful of tissues from her bag to help Sonia mop up. The letter could have fallen out then.

If she was to find it before anyone else, she needed to get to work before the Alexandra hummed into life. She supposed she could easily get the lab to send her a replacement copy. But that wouldn't help the confidentiality problem. A promise was a promise. If she didn't find it… If she didn't locate it *at once*, she'd have to inform Elliott. The thought of that made her feel slightly sick.

After that first meeting in the café—even before then, in fact, when she'd first laid eyes on him—she'd recognised he had a chill factor. Even his name, seen for the first time on her original birth certificate, had had a cold clink of reality to it. At eighteen, when the law had allowed, she'd gone through the procedures of finding out her birth parents' names out of curiosity, but probably would never have acted on the information. She doubted if she'd have contacted him at all, if it hadn't been for that Tuesday, exactly six weeks ago.

She'd been standing at the reception desk, checking a patient's file, when someone had approached the desk and said to Cindy, 'Elliott Fraser. I've brought Matthew for his check-up.'

Sophy's heart had jarred to a standstill. In a breathless kind of slow motion she'd looked up and seen him for the first time. Her father.

He was in his late forties, his hair already silver. He looked smooth and well-heeled, the image of a successful businessman. His eyes were a cold slate-grey, not like hers at all, and as he'd talked to Cindy his gaze hadn't warmed or changed in any way. Though Sophy had stared and stared to try to find a resemblance, she hadn't been able to see any.

There had to be one, though. People could hardly ever see like-nesses to themselves. She supposed she might take after her poor mother, who, according to the records, had died from contracting meningitis, but there should still be points of resemblance with her father.

Her glance had fallen then on the four-year-old at Elliott Fraser's side. He had the most endearing little solemn face. In a rush of con-flicted emotion she'd realised he was her half-brother.

How strange to see some of the actual people in the world who shared her blood, her genes. Even perhaps, if she were lucky, things in common. Though she'd loved her adoptive parents, they had a much older daughter in England from Bea's first marriage, and

Sophy had sometimes had the feeling she was being compared to her. Lauren was good at maths and science. While Sophy liked them, too, she preferred the arts. Lauren had done medicine, while Sophy had chosen to study child language development. Lauren went hiking and shinning up mountainsides, while Sophy liked growing things and browsing through bookshops.

Soon after Sophy had turned eighteen, it was as though Henry and Bea felt they'd discharged their responsibility towards their adopted child, for, even though there'd been lots of teary regrets and one long visit, they'd emigrated back to England to be with Lauren, Bea's *real* daughter, when she started her family.

Sophy often thought that if only she'd had brothers and sisters, she mightn't have missed her parents so badly. *Still* be missing them. That little brother…

As she remembered his big brown eyes her heart made a surge of pleasure, though it was tinged with concern. He'd been so sweet, but she'd had the most overwhelming instinct that he was lonely. Afterwards, going over and over the encounter in her mind, it had struck her clinical brain that, while Elliott Fraser had waited in Reception with him, he hadn't made one single eye contact with his son. There were books and toys for the children to investigate while they waited, but Matthew had sat all hunched up on the seat beside his father, as if hedged into his own little world. Elliott hadn't spoken to him once.

She saw that often in the clinic. Parents who didn't understand that their communication with their child was crucial. She wished there were some way she could help Matthew. Dreaming about it, she was so deep in thought that by the time she disembarked at Circular Quay she realised she hadn't noticed the early morning sights and smells of the harbour once in the entire trip. In Macquarie Street, she broke into a run, not easy in a pencil-slim skirt.

Thank goodness Security had already unlocked the building's heavy glass doors. Once inside, she pressed the button for the lift, but then decided she couldn't spare the time it took for the creaking cage to descend, and took the stairs instead.

The great domed skylight let in the morning, lighting the tiers of galleries where the doctors had their rooms. Tall, stained-glass windows at either end of the building tinctured the weak morning light with the faintest hues of rose and lavender.

Few people were in evidence this early, although the rich fragrance of coffee as she sprinted past the second gallery, mingled with the aromas rising up from the basement café, suggested that Millie, her friend and colleague, was there already, establishing herself in her new room.

Millie's old room was right next door to hers. It was bound to be unlocked, waiting to be refurbished. If she didn't find the envelope in the mothers' room, or even the washroom, it would have to still be safe in there.

At the top of the stairs she paused to regain her breath, and was faced with the sight of Millie's door, firmly shut. With a shock she saw a new sign emblazoned on it.

Connor O'Brien.

The words leaped out at her, bold and alive like a confrontation.

Connor O'Brien. Who was Connor O'Brien?

She flew along to the ladies' room, praying Security had unlocked it. To her relief the heavy mahogany door gave at once. Turning first to the washroom, she pushed through the swing door and scanned all the wash units, checked the bins, then strode through to the innermost room and peered into all the cubicles. Nothing.

Disappointing, but no surprise. The odds were still on the mothers' room.

She hurried across the tiny foyer, swung open the door to the mothers' room and was brought to a sudden standstill. For a confused instant she was confronted by what looked like a dark pillar shimmering in the white-tiled space, until she blinked and her vision cleared.

It was a man.

Naked to the waist, he was tall and lean, with strongly muscled arms and pitch-black hair. He was standing at the sink, his face half covered with shaving cream. A jacket and shirt were draped over a briefcase at his feet. His powerful torso was tanned, as if he'd spent real time in the sun, and as he performed his task small ripples disturbed the sleek, satin skin of his back.

His feet were as firmly planted on the floor of the mothers' room as if they had every right to be there. Didn't the man have a bathroom?

As he leaned further in she caught a glimpse of an angry, jagged scar across the ribs on his right side. A breathless sensation shook her, like the moment of sudden uplift on a ferris wheel. The door escaped from her paralysed fingers just as he was laying bare a swathe of smooth, bronzed cheek. His hand halted in mid-swipe, and in the mirror his gaze collided with hers.

His eyes were dark, deeper than the night, and heavy-lidded, fringed with black lashes beneath strong black brows. What grabbed at her, though, and shook up her insides, was their expression.

At that first instant of connection a sardonic gleam had shot through them. As if he'd recognised her.

Except… She didn't know him. Why should he recognise her?

He half turned and she caught a glimpse of his profile, a devastating sweep of forehead and long straight nose. Then he faced her full on and…

Gorgeous. Even half coated with foam, strength and masculine assurance declared themselves in the symmetrical bone structure of his lean, handsome face.

'Hi. Connor O'Brien.'

His voice was deep, with a rich, smooth texture. A smattering of dark whorled hair on his powerful chest invited her mesmerised gaze to follow its tapering path down beneath his belt buckle to…somewhere.

'Oh, er…er…hi. Sorry.' She backed out again into the foyer.

Connor looked after the closing door with some amusement. He began to regret postponing checking into a hotel. The last thing he needed was to alert Miss Sophy Woodruff to the suddenness of his arrangements. But who could have guessed she'd be so early to work?

He felt an intrigued little buzz in his veins. For a first glimpse, she had been nothing like he'd expected. Big soft eyes and sensitive, passionate mouths didn't go with tough little operators.

Unless, of course, they were her stock-in-trade. Perfect for sucking in middle-aged pigeons.

Outside in the foyer, Sophy tried to unscramble her brain. Whew. It took a few seconds to get the chest image out of her mind. Who needed to watch reruns of *Die Hard* with men like him around?

But, for goodness' sake, who could do any kind of a decent search in the presence of a semi-naked man? He was a damned nuisance. The cheek of him, treating the ladies' room like his own private en suite, even if it was barely six thirty.

And why, now she came to think of it, had she given ground? Whose rooms were they? If any of her fellow members of the Avengers netball team had been present, they'd have been yelling, 'Attack. Attack. Evict the intruder.'

She braced herself, and walked back in.

He was buttoning his shirt. Too late, though. That first impression was already seared into her brain. He might just as well have emerged dripping from a plunge in a weedy pond, his shirt clinging and transparent, for all the good it was doing him now.

At the sound of her step he flickered a glance over her from beneath his dark lashes. She knew that look. It was the hunter's assessment of her curves and sexual availability, as automatic to wolves and other male beasts as breathing.

'This is the mothers' room,' she asserted. His dark eyes sharpened beneath their dark lashes, and a sudden tension in the room seemed to affect her voice with an unwelcome throatiness. 'In case you didn't know.'

'I did know.' He rinsed his razor under the tap and gave it a couple of shakes. She waited for some sign he'd received the hint, but he resumed shaving with cool unconcern.

So who was he, *what* was he, that Millie had been obliged to make way for him? He didn't look like any of the doctors she knew.

She made a quick survey of the floor and surfaces. The cleaners had already done their work by the time she'd come in yesterday evening, but someone else might have picked the letter up after she'd left and thought it was rubbish. She glanced about for the bin and spotted it tucked under the sink. Directly in line with the man's long, elegantly shod feet.

Right. She straightened her shoulders, cleared her throat and stated with cool authority, 'Look, I'm sorry, but I'm afraid you'll have to finish that up somewhere else. There is a men's room further along.' She opened the door and held it wide with graceful, though determined, insistence.

Seconds ticked by, until she began to wonder if he'd even heard what she'd said, then he flashed her a lazy, long-lashed glance. 'I don't think so.'

To her intense indignation he remained as immovable as a tree trunk, continuing to scrape the foam from his handsome jaw as if he had all the time in the world. After a charged second in which her brain was jostled by a million incredulous thoughts about calling the police or the state emergency services for back-up, he had the nerve to add, 'No need to panic.'

Panic. Who was panicking? Even if such tall, dark sexiness was a rarity at the Alexandra, Sophy Woodruff was perfectly well able to deal with it, in the mothers' room or anywhere else.

Forced to, if she didn't want to look like an idiot, she let the door swing shut, as, without the slightest interest in her wishes, he started on the moustache area. Naturally her eyes were drawn to watch the delicate operation. Before she could properly drag them away, he paused and the corners of his mouth edged up a little.

'I'll be out of your way in a few seconds. Don't let my presence make you nervous.'

His voice might have risen from some bottomless inner well of chocolate liqueur, so appealing its deep timbre was to the clinically trained ear. Or would have been, if it hadn't been for the subtle mockery in it.

'Nervous?' She gave a careless laugh. 'My only concern is that at any minute now mothers may need to come in here to nurse their babies.'

He glanced at his watch. 'At six thirty-six?'

'Well, certainly.' It was only a bit of a lie. In truth, the clinics didn't usually open until seven-thirty, but in an emergency they very well might open earlier. 'There could be early appointments. I think you should be aware that this room is intended for the sole use of mothers.'

'Ah.' A gleam lit his dark eyes. 'Then in that case we'd both better leave.'

Without waiting for her reply, he turned back to his reflection. Shaving foam outlined his mouth, highlighting its chiselled perfection, the top lip straight and stern, the lower one sensual in that ruthless, masculine way. Mouths could be deceptive, though. In terms of kissing, sometimes even the most promising lips could end up being a disappointment. It all depended on the proficiency of the kisser. And the chemistry with the kissee.

Connor O'Brien's razor hand arrested in mid-air and his eyes locked with hers.

'Missed a bit, have I?'

The depth of knowing amusement in his glance burnt her to the soles of her feet.

'Pardon?' she said, forcing herself to hold that mocking gaze and ignore the pinkening tide flooding to her hairline. 'Are you asking for my advice? I'm afraid I can't help you. I know very little about men's hair-growth problems.'

With supreme dignity, she turned away and made an emphatic effort to search.

Connor smiled to himself, noting Miss Sophy Woodruff's apparent sensitivity with a pleasurable leap of surprise. It was rare to draw a blush in a woman, and strangely stirring. If she was the cold opportunist Sir Frank suspected, her ability to colour up was quite an accomplishment.

She was paused now in the middle of the room, making a slow twirl in search of something, giving him ample opportunity to observe her undulating curves, long slim legs and slender, graceful neck. He wouldn't have expected Elliott Fraser to risk everything over a scrubber, but that grainy photo had hardly done her justice.

He wondered what she was searching for.

'I humbly apologise for intruding on your sacred female space,' he said, in a bid to tempt her to turn his way again, the better to drink in more of her oval face. Luminous blue eyes—or had her lavender shirt turned them violet?—fringed by thick black lashes. Rosy lips against pale creamy skin. Enough to make any man's mouth water. 'No threat intended,' he added soothingly.

Sophy sent him a sardonic glance. A man caught in flagrante shouldn't try to flirt his way out of trouble. She wished now she'd called Security and had him thrown out.

'Do you usually prefer the women's to the gents'?'

Beneath his black lashes his eyes glinted. The air she breathed suddenly felt charged with dangerous, high-voltage sparks.

'Nearly always. You know how it is. I like to network. And what better place to meet people?' His bold, dark gaze drifted from her mouth to her breasts, down to her legs and back again.

Skin cells scorched all the way to her ankles. She turned her back on him and bent to check the sofa where she'd sat yesterday, slipping her hand down behind the seat cushion and feeling around the perimeter.

There was nothing there except dusty lint. Hyper-conscious of *him*, she straightened up to skim the change table and benchtops. He was pretending to be engaged again on his task, but she wasn't deceived. He was tuned into her every move, or her name wasn't Sophy Woodruff.

Or…or whatever it was.

She eyed the leather case beside him on the draining board. He might, just might, have found the envelope and be intending to hand it in. 'Er…' It was a stretch now at this late stage, but she tried to crank some goodwill into her voice. 'Have you by any chance— found a letter in here?'

'A letter.' His expressive brows gave a quizzical twitch while he considered. 'This seems an unusual place to expect a mail delivery. It isn't a covert letter-drop for the CIA, now, is it?'

That sexy, teasing note again in his deep voice. And there was something hard underneath, almost as if he didn't believe in her sincerity.

In an effort to show she was in earnest, she ignored his tone. 'It's not a delivery. I've misplaced an envelope. I think it may have dropped from my bag somewhere. Over there where I was sitting, or…'

'What sort of envelope?'

'Just a plain, buff-coloured… You know, with a window in it, like—' Like any official communication to Miss Violet Woodruff, she was about to say, until it occurred to her then how ridiculous it was, having to describe it. How many envelopes was he likely to have found? 'Look, does it matter what kind it is? Have you or haven't you found it?'

In her frustration, she might have sounded a tad impatient, because he turned from the mirror and directed the full force of his dark, shimmering gaze on her.

'I don't know if I should answer that. It would depend to whom such an envelope was addressed.'

She felt a small shock, as if she'd come up against an unexpected concrete wall, but said, as pleasantly as she could, 'Well, obviously, it's addressed to me.'

'Ah. So you say.' The infuriating man had finished shaving at last, and turned to wash his razor under the tap. 'But, then, who are you?'

It was clear he was toying with her. 'I'm—' She drew herself up to her full five-seven in heels and asserted, 'You know, Security in this building is very strict. They wouldn't tolerate your intrusion in here.'

'Ah. Now, that's where you're wrong. The fact is, it was the Security guy with the freckles who unlocked these rooms for me, since the Gents is having some sort of problem with the pipes.'

'Oh.' Nonplussed, she took a second before she managed a come-back. 'Well, it's a pity he didn't explain that that sink you're using is intended for nursing mothers who want to make themselves a cup of tea. I hope you give it a good wash when you're finished.'

The man's eyes gleamed, but he continued, musing, 'Not all states feel the need to pursue this rigid segregation of the sexes. Take France, for example. A French woman visiting the mothers' room in, say, the Louvre, would be very unlikely to feel threatened by the presence of a man shaving. Though, I suppose any woman who's not used to being around men…a woman, say, who's never watched a man shave…never been kissed, as the saying goes…'

Never been kissed. Was he trying to insult her? She hissed in a breath through her teeth. 'Look, all I want to know is if you found my envelope. If you *didn't*…'

He put on a bland expression. 'I think I might be able to help if you could be more specific. For instance, if you could give me some idea of the letter's likely contents…'

'What?' She stared at him in incredulity. 'Are you for real? Look, why can't you just *say*—?'

She broke off, shaking her head in disbelief as he bent to splash his face, his composure unruffled.

Her heart started to thud. He must have found it. Why else was he being so obstructive? She breathed deeply for several seconds, wondering how to go about extracting the truth from him. Often she could sense things in people, but in his case she was aware only of an implacable resistance. Despair gripped her. What was left for her to try? An appeal to him as a human being?

He reached for a paper towel and turned to her, patting his face dry.

'Are you sure—absolutely sure—you didn't find it?' Despite an attempt to sound calm she knew the plea in her voice revealed her desperation, loud and clear.

He crumpled the paper towel and dropped it in the bin. Then he slipped a purple silk tie under his collar and tied it, practice in the fluid movements of his lean, tanned fingers. At the same time he turned to appraise her with his dark, intelligent gaze. Drops of moisture sparkled on his black lashes.

'It's beginning to sound like a very important letter.'

'It is. That is—' She checked herself. The more she talked up the importance of the letter, the more likely he would be to read it if he found it. Just supposing he hadn't already. 'No, no, well, it's not really. It's only important to me. Not to anyone else.'

He nodded in apparent understanding, his sardonic face suddenly grave. Perhaps she'd misjudged him. Perhaps he could even be sympathetic. Although, how safe was it to trust him? If he could only be serious for a minute…

She watched him shrug on his jacket, then slip the leather case into his briefcase, all the while continuing her theme of playing the letter down. 'It's nothing really. Just a small—private thing.'

'Ah.' His dark lashes flickered down. 'A love letter.'

'No,' she snapped, goaded. 'Not a love letter. Look, why can't you be serious? Why can't you give me a straight answer?'

He sighed. 'All right. How about this one? I haven't found your letter. You can search me if you like.' He spread his hands in invitation, offering her the pockets of his jacket, his trousers, then as she glared at him in disbelief he thrust his briefcase at her. 'Go on. Search.'

As if she could. She wanted to snatch the briefcase from him and whack him with it. But even without touching it, she knew there was nothing of hers inside. He was tormenting her, when all he'd had to do was to tell her in the first place…

'Do you know,' she said, an angry tremor in her low voice, 'you are a very rude and aggravating man?'

'I do know,' he said ruefully, wickedness in the dark eyes beneath his black lashes. 'I'm ashamed of myself.'

She felt her blood pressure rise as he moved closer until his broad chest was a bare few inches from her breasts. The clean male scent of him, the masculine buzz of his aura, plunged her normally tranquil pulse into chaos. She became suffocatingly conscious of the nearness of the vibrant, muscled body lurking beneath his clothes.

The dark gaze dwelling on her face grew sensual and turned her blood into a molten, racing torrent. 'And do *you* know that you're a very uptight little chick? You should learn to relax.'

His sexy mouth was uncomfortably near, and, involuntarily, her own dried. She glowered at him, anger rendering her unable to breathe or speak.

He flicked her cheek. 'I'll let you know if I find your letter.' His bold gaze travelled down her throat to the neck of her shirt, then back. 'You know, with those eyes your name should be Violet.' He turned and strolled to the door, and while she stood there, the cool touch of his fingers still burning on her skin, it swung shut behind him. Then the enormity of what he'd said hit her like a train. The incredible words resounded in her ears.

He knew her name.

He'd known it all along. That had been no coincidence.

But how could he know it? How, unless he'd found her letter?

CHAPTER THREE

SOPHY strode along the gallery to the children's clinic. Connor O'Brien's door was closed, but she had to steel herself to walk past it and breathe the air he was infecting with his intolerable masculine game-playing. He was probably in there now, gloating over her DNA profile.

Although, what could it possibly mean to him? What could he *do* with it? Apart from post it on the Internet. Take it to the papers. Contact Elliott…

She shut her eyes and tried to breathe calmly. The man could be a blackmailer. He looked bad, with that mocking dark gaze and that sardonic mouth. Just remembering his refusal to take her seriously made her blood boil all over again. She wished she'd said something clever and cutting enough to douse that insolent amusement in his eyes.

She used her pass key to unlock the clinic, relieved that neither Cindy, their receptionist, nor Bruce, the paediatrician, had arrived yet, praying that against the odds someone wonderful had found the letter and popped it through the mail slot. But no such luck. In her office she plunged into a frenzied search, her desk, her drawers, all around the children's table and chairs, the armchairs for parents, only confirming what she already knew—she'd lost it *after* she'd left yesterday.

Millie was her last resort. She'd spent a good hour in there yesterday, helping her friend pack up her files. Fingers crossed, she phoned her, but again her luck was out. Amidst all her files and books, Millie had been in too much of an uproar to find anything, let alone something so ordinary and unobtrusive as an envelope.

She slumped down in her chair. Perhaps she should alert Elliott, but she wasn't ready to give up yet. He'd seemed so paranoid at the idea of the news getting out. Not that she could blame him altogether. Her existence had come as a complete shock to him. She pitied him for what he must have gone through when he found out. Anyone—*anyone* would have been upset.

She tried to crush down a nasty feeling at how he might react when he knew the letter was out of her hands. Then, with some relief, she remembered he said he'd be out of town for a week, and brightened a little. At least that gave her a bit of breathing space. He might not have even received his copy yet.

And, honestly, what was the worst that could happen to him if the news got out? Thousands of people had given up their children for adoption, for all sorts of reasons. It was hardly such a shocking scandal anymore. His wife should be capable of understanding something that had happened twenty-three years ago.

And it wasn't as if she wasn't an independent adult. She hoped she'd made it absolutely crystal clear that it wouldn't *cost* him anything to invite her into his life—their lives. Only a bit of friendship. Not a relationship, exactly. She knew she couldn't expect that.

But there was no denying her disappointment. Elliott's utter dismay when she'd made that first contact had been almost tangible. He'd tried to disguise it with his smooth manners, but she'd been able to sense how he truly felt. In the subsequent meetings, in the coffee shop and the bar, he'd seemed more concerned to find out who she might have told rather than how she'd spent her life to date, while *she*...

Her heart had been so full, so brimming over with joy and hope, she'd wanted to know everything about him. And Matthew.

But she felt sure, when someone got to know him, he was a wonderful person. When he got used to the idea, he would come round to seeing the fantastic side of having a daughter.

Restlessly she got up and started tweaking some brown-edged leaves from her geraniums on the window ledge. She hadn't felt such confusion for years, not since Henry and Bea had told her they were staying on in England for a bit. Possibly for ever. She lifted her gaze to the Botanical Gardens across the street, wishing she could go across right now, before she saw the first of the children on her morning's list. Somehow the soothing essence of those cool, leafy pathways always managed to soak into her like balm.

Connor O'Brien was to blame for this turmoil. A wave of puzzlement swept through her. What was wrong with him? Why had he been so mocking, almost *distrustful* of her?

His behaviour had been so arrogant, so callous and indifferent, as if her anxiety had been a joke. And as for that crack about her never having been kissed…

Of course she had. Countless times. He'd only been teasing, using a typical male ploy to start a flirty conversation, unless he'd been suggesting… A chilling possibility crept in. If, by some quirk of fate, a woman still happened to be a virgin, surely that minor detail wasn't obvious to people? Could there be something about her that flagged her status to the world?

And if so, what? Could it be her clothes? Her conversation? The way she walked?

She'd never thought it worth worrying about before. It was just— the way things had turned out for her.

It wasn't that she hadn't had opportunities. Plenty of men had been keen to relieve her of it. And she had no philosophical objections to sex. In fact, she fully believed that every woman should drink deeply from the cup of life, although the values Henry and Bea had instilled in her had quietly insisted that the drinker should be in love. And there was the little matter of trust. She'd tried a few tentative sips once or twice, but for some reason the trust factor had always intruded and she'd stalled at a certain point.

Leah and Zoe, her flatmates, called her a late bloomer. Sooner or later, they declared, some ruthless hunk would send her completely overboard and she'd plunge right in. And that was where she needed to beware, because someone as dreamy and impulsive as Sophy Woodruff was at risk of a broken heart.

If she wanted to land a man, she needed to do her research, they'd said. Find a solid prospect with financial security and a career trajectory, and plan a campaign.

'But what if we have nothing in common?' she'd argued.

The answer was stern and unequivocal. 'Plan a campaign. *Build* things in common.'

What Zoe and Leah didn't understand—well, they did, but they scoffed about it—was that she had dreams. And dreams didn't go with campaigns. In fact, she preferred to rely on her instincts about people, though she couldn't always, she had to admit. She had been mistaken more than once, sometimes quite spectacularly. But she'd known definitely at once that those boys she'd turned down just didn't have the chemistry, and never, ever would.

As for her needing to become more proactive, with a plan and some cold, hard strategy, she doubted she could bring that off. Campaigns weren't her style. In the situation she was in right now, though, some cool, ruthless strategy was definitely warranted.

She felt a little shiver of apprehension.

There was only one thing for it. Whatever it took, she would have to find a way to seize her letter back. She couldn't allow Connor O'Brien to ruin her chance to know her father before it had even begun. And he wouldn't win any future encounter with her, either, dammit. He'd better learn that, kissed or unkissed, Sophy Woodruff was a force to be reckoned with.

Somehow, if it killed her, she would find a way into his office.

It gave her an eerie feeling to realise that at this very second he might be on the other side of her wall, gazing out at the very same view.

Connor frowned out across the treetops, beyond the Gardens, to where a strip of Walsh Bay glimmered under a hot blue sky. It occurred to him that not so very far away, as the crow flew, he owned a house. Most of his father's things had been auctioned for charity, as became the possessions of the extremely wealthy, but it might do, especially as it wasn't too far from the haunts of Elliott Fraser. He was sure he'd left some of his law books there. Slightly outdated perhaps, but he could pick up some of the current publications later. It might be interesting to see what had changed this side of his old profession.

He stepped back from the window and gazed appreciatively around at the high-ceilinged rooms with their ornate cornices. If he'd been setting up for real, he couldn't have found a more pleasing location.

He glanced at his watch. Organise a car, then take some time to pick up his books and some stationery supplies before the office furnishings were delivered. Consider his next encounter with Sophy Woodruff....

His pulse rate quickened. He wondered what the letter was she'd been searching for. The anxiety in those stunning eyes had seemed genuine enough. With her sweet low voice, the ready flush washing into her cheek, she'd seemed amazingly soft, too soft to be any of the things Sir Frank suspected. But he was too hardened a case to be sucked in by appearances. Women in the profession could be superb actresses...

Whatever she was searching for, his challenge would be to find it first.

He remembered the fire that had flashed in those blue eyes when he'd touched her, and his blood stirred. He could so enjoy a worthy protagonist.

* * *

At lunchtime, on her way down to the basement deli, Sophy saw Connor O'Brien assisting some workmen to manoeuvre a handsome rosewood bookshelf through his door. She grimaced to herself. No doubt he needed it for storing other people's private documents.

She queued at the deli for a salad sandwich, but instead of taking it to her usual picnic spot in the Gardens, headed back upstairs to finish some of the morning's reports. As she reached the top of the last flight her stomach flipped in excitement.

Connor's door was standing half open.

Her imagination leaped to the possibilities. The workmen must have gone to pick up their next load. Had the arrogant beast gone with them?

Except that would be too good to be true. Surely he wouldn't leave his office unlocked and unattended?

With a thudding heart, she slowed her pace, and as she reached his door hesitated, pretending to search for something in her bag. She could hear no sound from within. All she could see in the slice of reception office visible through the half-open door was an empty expanse of carpet and the corner of the built-in reception desk.

He could be in the inner room, though, skulking. She hovered there, straining her ears, trying to guess if anyone was inside. If he was in there, she reasoned, she should be able to sense his presence. A quick glance along the gallery revealed a couple of people waiting for the lift at the other end. She closed her eyes and listened, but the air seemed flat and empty.

Voices floated up to her from below. She darted across and looked over the balustrade. There were people on the stairs to the lower levels, but no sign of Connor O'Brien. And the lift must have arrived without the workmen, for the waiting people were now stepping into it.

For the moment, the coast seemed to be clear.

It was too good a chance to lose. She made a small precaution-ary knock, then waited with her heart thumping fit to burst. Nothing disturbed the stillness. Feeling as guilty as a thief, she cast a last furtive glance about, then slipped inside.

Familiar with the layout, she sensed immediately that the entire suite, including both offices and the tiny tea-room inside, were unoccupied. She ventured through the connecting door into the larger room. Already Millie's comfortable presence had gone. The place had a different feel, as if it had been given over to some sterner god.

Daylight streamed in through the tall windows, and with it the view her office shared of the Botanical Gardens and the strip of harbour beyond. A laptop sat on a heavy rosewood desk beside a stack of new stationery—cardboard folder files, packaged paper and a selection of office equipment. The bookshelves were bare, a large tea chest of books beside them waiting to be unpacked. She tilted her head and read a couple of the titles upside down. *Policy and Practice of Human Rights Law. International Human Rights.*

She felt disconcerted. Connor O'Brien was a lawyer?

How ironic. If he was so concerned about human rights, what was he doing stealing people's private letters? For a second she experienced a doubt. It hardly made sense. Could she have leaped to the wrong conclusion and lost her letter somewhere else?

Even visualising the envelope made a hot and cold sensation of the most unmistakable immediacy sweep over her, as though all the tiny hairs on her body were standing on end. Her overwhelming instinct told her it was close by. If she closed her eyes, she could practically feel the texture of the paper in her hands. Without a doubt she knew it had to be here in this room.

The question was where?

A new filing cabinet stood within easy reach of the desk. She glanced over her shoulder at the door and, ignoring some warning prickles in her nape, tried the top drawer. It sounded empty, but it was locked. They were all locked. She felt a surge of excitement.

Why would he lock the filing cabinet if he had nothing worth hiding? She looked around for the keys. She tried the desk drawers first, but, finding them empty, turned to survey the room. Her eye fell on a briefcase, leaning up against the leg of his desk chair.

Ah. A thrill of guilty excitement shivered down her spine.

Should she?

She vacillated for a moment, but with the seconds ticking away it was no time for squeamishness. Her pulse drumming in her ears, she whisked the briefcase up onto the desk, pushing aside stationery to make room, and unzipped the main compartment intended for the laptop. It was empty, apart from a couple of memory sticks.

Increasingly conscious of the possibility of the workmen's return, she made a hasty search of the other compartments. Her letter wasn't in any of them, nor any keys. In fact, the case contained nothing except for a few odds and ends for the computer. That was when she noticed Connor O'Brien's jacket, slung on the back of his chair.

Having sunk this deep into crime, rifling a personal jacket didn't seem much more of a stretch.

Gingerly, suspense creeping up her spine, she slipped her hands into the side pockets, and came up with nothing. She had no greater luck with the breast pocket, although her fingers detected a bulge through the fabric. She turned the jacket to the inside and tried the inset pocket. Her heart bounded in her chest. There was no envelope in there. Only a passport.

She slipped it out, then put it straight back in. This would be an unforgivable invasion of the man's privacy. But then, how concerned was he about respecting hers?

With a bracing breath, she squashed down her scruples and took out the alluring little red book.

Probably it was her imagination, but the covers felt warm to her touch, as if the book vibrated with some vital energy. It was such a temptation. Surely it wouldn't hurt to examine the photo. Almost at once she gave in, opening straight to the ID page to be faced with Connor O'Brien.

She might have known. Other people took ghastly mugshots, but not him. She stared, riveted, as his face looked out at her, stern and unsmiling, but still with the faint possibility of amusement breaking out on his sardonic mouth. He was thirty-four, according to his birthdate. She flicked to the back pages, and widened her eyes in surprise. Connor was a frequent traveller. And a *recent* one, going by the last stamp in the book. He'd only just arrived in the country.

She'd heard of workaholics, but this was an extreme case, surely, if he came to work straight off a plane without going home first to shave. Unable to resist one more look at his picture, she flipped back to the identity page. Was it her imagination, or were his eyes piercing her now with that infuriating mockery as if he knew what she was doing and could see right through her?

Her heart suddenly thumping too fast, she snapped the book shut. She held it between her palms, swept by a confused mixture of conflicting instincts about Connor O'Brien. They couldn't all be true. Was she going insane?

She gave an alarmed start as the sound of approaching voices alerted her that she was about to be caught red-handed, and the passport slipped from her fingers.

She dived to pick it up as bumps and grunts began to issue from the reception office, suggestive of several men hefting some bulky piece of furniture through a narrow aperture.

In her haste to slot the little book into the pocket, she knocked the stationery pile askew, and sent manilla folders sliding across the desk and onto the floor.

She dropped to her knees, and as she scrabbled to gather the files and stack them back on the desk the activity outside ceased. Her heart nearly seized as she caught sight of the briefcase. Quickly she dashed it onto the floor. For a panicked instant she considered hiding in the tea-room, then dismissed the action as cowardly.

She could do this, she thought, her heart slamming into her ribs.

She'd just brazen it out. She straightened up and faced the door, steeled for the worst.

There was a brief exchange of conversation outside. She was straining to hear what was being said when the door to the room burst open. At almost the identical moment her horrified gaze fell on the passport, still lying on the corner of the desk.

She snatched it up, whipping it behind her back just as Connor strode in. When he saw her, he stopped short, an initial flare of astonishment in his dark eyes changing nearly at once to cynicism. Almost as if catching her there was no real surprise.

Without a word he stepped past her, seized a pen from the desk, and turned back to the outer room, where he signed something on a clipboard presented to him by one of the delivery men.

With no time to return the passport to his jacket, and nowhere to hide it, she popped it down the front of her shirt, just as Connor turned to stroll slowly and purposefully back into his office.

If he saw her surreptitious movement, he didn't show it. He shut the door gently behind him, then paused to examine her, his black eyebrows raised.

He looked taller, grimmer and more authoritative when he was annoyed. It was harder to imagine him plunging through the pond.

No. No, it wasn't.

Her mouth became uncomfortably dry, and she smoothed her skirt with moistening palms.

He didn't appear to be imagining her in as favourable a light. His speculative gaze swept over her while she waited in an anguish of suspense, realising from the hard glint in his eyes he wasn't about to let her off lightly.

'Did you want something?' His deep voice was polite, with just a tinge of incredulity lapping at its edges.

As if he didn't know. The sheer duplicity of the man.

She tried to assume a cool, poised demeanour. 'Oh, look, er, I should apologise. I probably shouldn't have walked in. I came to—

speak to you. The door was open, so I just—' she made a breezy gesture '—wandered in.' Her voice wobbled a little, but she kept her head high and forced herself to keep meeting his eyes, all the time conscious of her pulse ticking like a time bomb.

His eyes flicked to his desk, over the once rigidly neat pile of stationery, now listing dangerously to one side, and on—to her conscious eyes at least—to the neon-flashing space where she'd rested the briefcase.

In a brilliant move inspired by adrenaline, she did the only possible thing, and sat on the desk in the telltale space, stretching a hand back so she could lean, and once again knocking over the wonky pile.

'Oh, damn,' she said, trying to sound careless, 'that's the second time I've done that.'

Connor O'Brien didn't look fooled. His acute dark eyes slid over her in sardonic appreciation. She grew uncomfortably conscious of her breasts and legs, accentuated by her posture, and hoped the red passport didn't blaze through her shirt.

'What can I help you with, Sophy?'

She smiled, but her sexual sensors, to say nothing of the others, were all madly oscillating on panic alert. Somehow, though, the danger she was in gave her a reckless sort of courage. She hadn't spent lonely years of her life watching old black-and-white movie reels into the small hours for nothing. She knew how Lana Turner would have played this scene.

'Ah, so you've found out my name,' she said throatily, crossing her legs.

His glinting gaze flicked to them. 'I described you to the Security guy. He had no trouble recognising you.'

Something in his voice told her the conversation he'd had with the man had been a loaded one. She could just imagine the sort of things they'd said about her. If his passport hadn't been burning a hole in her midriff, she might have been incensed. As it was, her major concern for the moment, apart from escaping unscathed, was how she was to return it to its pocket. It was one thing to be suspected of snooping, another to leave behind glaring evidence.

What if he accused her of stealing? He could have her up before the courts. Her boss would be forced to sack her. Perhaps, though, if she owned up and produced the passport at once...

She examined Connor's face for signs of softening, but his eyebrows were heavy and forbidding, his mouth and jaw stern.

Lana would have known what to do. If ever there was a man who needed beguiling, here was the man. Her skirt had ridden up a little on her thigh, and she discreetly tugged it down.

Connor O'Brien didn't miss the movement. He prowled closer and stood looking down at her with his harsh, uncompromising gaze. 'Breaking and entering is a criminal offence.' She noticed his glance flick to her mouth. 'What were you hoping to steal?'

Her heart made a scared lurch at the '*s*' word. Somehow, owning up lost its attractiveness as an option.

'Steal? That's ridiculous.' She fluttered her lashes in denial. 'It was hardly breaking and entering... You left your door wide-open, and I came in to talk to you. Simple as that.'

He looked unconvinced. 'I should hand you over to that Security guy and make his day.'

'Oh, why? For coming in for a chat?'

'A *chat*.' His lip curled in disbelief. 'About what?'

She wished he wouldn't use that sceptical tone. It was rich, this distrust he had of her, when he was the one who stole people's confidential DNA reports.

'The weather,' she said, rolling her eyes. 'What else?'

She slid off the desk so she could bring more height to the exchange, but standing before Connor only seemed to illustrate how slight and insubstantial five feet seven of guilty woman was in comparison with six feet three of hard, cynical man. Still, after the way *he'd* behaved, his outraged morality act was too much to swallow.

'I felt a bit sorry about not being so friendly this morning.' She stretched languidly, then sashayed towards the door, casting him a long Lana-esque glance over her shoulder. 'But I see now that my first instincts about you were correct.'

She had just grasped the door knob when she felt a big powerful bulk stride up behind her. A lean hand closed firmly over hers.

'No, you don't, sweetheart. Not yet.'

She could feel his hot breath on her neck. As his raw masculine proximity washed over her, accelerating her pulse into a mad racing turmoil, it homed in on her that, while *she* might have been playing Lana Turner, he was no two-dimensional Hollywood hero on the silver screen. He was a big, dangerous, flesh-and-blood man, and he wasn't confined to a script.

Heat emanated from his body. She turned to face him, her back against the door, barely able to keep her rapid breathing under control, panting like a marathon runner. Her blood throbbed with a tense excitement. Still, as sexy as he looked with his black brows bristling, his intelligent dark eyes scouring her face, she reminded herself that he was the man who'd stolen her letter. It was imperative that she keep her wits about her.

She made an attempt to ignore the major chemical reaction effervescing inside her, and stiffened her spine.

He stepped back a little to study her, frowning, his dark eyes burning with a curious intensity. 'Empty your pockets.'

In spite of her bravado, she felt her cheeks flame with the insult. 'I don't have any.'

A dark gleam lit his eyes. 'Ah. Well, then, I'll have no choice but to search you.'

Her stomach lurched. The silkiness of his deep voice couldn't disguise the determination in the set of his chiselled jaw.

It was a seminal moment. If she allowed him to make the attempt, she was lost. His stern, masculine mouth, not so far away from hers, relaxed its unforgiving lines, as though Connor was enjoying his mastery of the situation. His mastery of *her*.

Suspense coiled her insides.

On a rush of adrenaline, she leaned back against the door, her breasts rising and falling, and breathed huskily, 'But…would you feel honourable about violating my person? A woman who's never been kissed?'

His eyes flickered over her face and throat. She could sense his hesitation, his struggle against temptation. It gave her such an exhilarating feeling to see that she could tempt him from his intent. And he *would* succumb, she realised with a thrilled, almost incredulous certainty, her heart thundering.

Beneath his black lashes his pupils flared like a hungry wolf's.

He curled his lean fingers under her jaw. 'That can be fixed,' he said. Then he brought his lips down on hers with deliberate, sensual purpose.

At that first firm touch, a fiery tingling sensation shot through her veins like an electric charge, and sent an immediate swell of warmth to her breasts.

A shudder roiled through Connor's tall frame, as with a gruff little sexy sound he increased the sizzling pressure and sent her blood temperature soaring.

She tried to remember he was her adversary, and made a half-hearted attempt to cool her response, but he drew her in closer. Then, like the cunning devil he was, he softened the kiss to clever, gentle persuasion, until the fire on her lips ignited her bloodstream and aroused all her secret, intimate places with erotic yearning.

Though he was a big, powerful man, he held her tenderly, his lean, tanned hands on her waist. His touch was so seductive that, instead of her putting up a sound resistance, her own hands went sliding across his ribs. Even through his shirt, the heat of his hard, vibrant body under her palms was so thrilling, she couldn't restrain herself from writhing with pleasure.

Just when she was ready to swoon at all the intoxicating sensations of hot, strong, tender man, he tempted her lips apart with his tongue.

The taste of him exploded in her senses like a sunburst. Faint tangs of coffee and toothpaste were overridden with another flavour, some arousing primitive essence that was surely unique to him. His devilish tongue slid through, teasing and stroking erotic tissues inside her mouth she hadn't been aware existed. The sheer pleasure of his artful, gliding tongue lit her with a fever that infected every little corner of her being.

Her insides went into involuntary meltdown. Boneless, she had to clutch at him for support.

And he was so satisfying to the touch. He was all hard muscle, bone and sinew, as strong and unyielding as steel. Through his shirt, the solid reality of him under her clinging hands felt *right*, and her breasts strained against her bra for—*something*.

As her brain swam in a drugged delirium the hot, panting hunger of desire stalked through her feverish body like a ravenous panther. She had little doubt Connor felt it, too, for on deepening the kiss he pulled her even harder against him, as though to experience more intensely her softness in arousing friction with his lean, sexy body.

His restless, seeking hands caressed her breasts, the curves of her waist and hips, and she burned for more. She let go of all her reservations about him and surrendered herself utterly. Lost in the escalating sensation, she hardly noticed a sharp little tweak of the shirt at her waist until she became aware of the scrape of his knuckles on the skin of her midriff. Then his hands came up to her shoulders, and he pushed her away.

The sudden cold shock left her gasping and adrift.

As she stood struggling to adjust to reality, her blood still heavy and inflamed, Connor stepped away a pace. He was breathing hard, his darkened eyes ablaze. An angry quirk curled his mouth. He held up his passport and waved it at her.

'Did you really think you'd get away with this?' The clipped words were like a face-slap.

'Oh. Oh, that.' Impossible, considering how flushed she must have been already, but she felt her ears grow hot enough to spontaneously combust. 'Look, I did intend to put it back, but you—you came in too soon.' As his expression impinged on her brain her breathless, husky voice grew more strained. 'I couldn't think of what else to do with it. Sorry.'

'*Sorry.*' Several conflicting emotions warred on his handsome face. Astonishment, bemusement and—judging by the compression of his stirringly sexy mouth—contempt. He gave a sardonic shrug. 'Well, I hope you were satisfied with what you discovered.'

Stung by his disdain, she was reminded of his callous behaviour when she'd been so anxious over her letter, the letter he'd *stolen*, and felt her own anger flare.

'Well, I'm not satisfied,' she snapped. 'And I won't be satisfied until I get my letter back.'

'What?' He stared at her, then his face changed and his dark eyes lit with amused comprehension. 'Oh, your *letter*. Of course.' To her absolute fury he had the insensitivity to laugh. 'Still searching for that, are you?' His smile slowly faded and his gaze softened as he read her hot, flushed face, her heaving breasts. 'Ah, but it was worth getting caught, though, don't you think?' He reached forward and brushed her mouth with his finger. 'Delicious, Sophy.' His deep voice was velvet with sensuality. 'You must come and search again.'

She felt the strongest desire to murder Connor O'Brien.

She turned on her heel and yanked open the door, and had to restrain herself to walk with dignity and not run. When she reached the clinic, she strode blindly past Reception without seeing a soul, then stalked through her room to the window, where she stood gasping in air and trying to cool her face.

She was in a confused daze for minutes, then thoughts finally seethed to the surface in her brain. She absolutely loathed that man. She would get her letter back. And she would make him *suffer*.

Later on, though, after she'd cooled down and had time to analyse her feelings, she realised her humiliation was not so much about being caught. She didn't feel as guilty as she should about breaking in. The circumstances had demanded a bold move and the opportunity had been too good to throw away. She didn't really even feel bad about the passport. That had merely been the result of an unfortunate sequence of events.

The thing that was tearing at her, eating her up, gnawing at her soul—was that kiss.

She covered her cheeks with her hands. If she hadn't responded to him… She felt herself grow hot all over again at the thought of her undeniable enthusiasm. She hadn't seemed able to help herself. And he… *He* had seemed equally involved during the—event. She couldn't forget, though, how quickly he'd regained his cool, while she'd still been so hot and aroused to the bitter end.

What was truly humiliating was not knowing why he'd kissed her.

Had it only been because he'd known she had the passport?

Or—because he'd wanted to?

Connor finished shelving his books and closed the glass doors. The latest developments in his field as they applied to the rules of war had been his daily practice for years. Now, seeing the tomes lined up so proudly, his curiosity was aroused about what might have changed in human rights practice on the domestic front. This would be a good opportunity to catch up.

He glanced about him with satisfaction. His short-term hired furniture looked quite impressive. He could almost imagine what it would be like to set up here for real, with Sophy Woodruff in the room next door.

She was a puzzle. If Sir Frank's suspicions had any foundation, she was the most unusual operative he'd ever encountered.

He made a wry grimace at himself, still getting over his astounding lapse of judgement in leaving his passport unsecured. All at once Sir Frank's warning about him reaching his use-by date had a prophetic ring to it.

He would have to assume she'd have noticed the difference in his passport, forcing him now to some further embroidery of his cover story. Still, the lapse could work in his favour. Only a man with nothing to hide left his office door unlocked.

He smiled to himself, remembering her petrified expression in the first instant he'd surprised her search. Her clear blue eyes, alight with mingled horror and shame—that hint of a laugh dying to break out.

The question was whether she was inept, or very, very clever.

Whatever she was searching for now assumed crucial dimensions. With her being prepared to risk being caught in his office, she had to be near desperate, although there was no doubt she'd played her role of nervous bravado to perfection.

Of course, she still might have done if she were Sir Frank's other possibility—a rapacious predator seeking to lift a besotted middle-aged man from the marital nest.

That wasn't how she'd tasted, though. His blood stirred at the memory of her response. Her surrender had felt genuine. Fresh, and sweet… He had to admit he'd surprised himself. It had been a long time since he'd come so close to losing control.

His instinct for self-preservation made a belated attempt to drag itself off the floor and assert its presence. He should never have done it. There was a price to pay for kissing sensitive women with soft, ripe lips. That sort of addiction could grow cruel.

Squaring his shoulders, he reminded himself of the rules taught to him in the hard school of grief and loss. He must never allow a woman into his life. His code must be absolute. No woman could ever cross the threshold of his domain, and whoever she was, however tempting, he would never enter hers. An occasional rendezvous in some anonymous hotel room, a partner who gave the minimum and expected nothing in return, were the most he could ever risk, for the woman's sake, as well as his own.

Connections, emotions, attachments—all off-limits. Fraught with every kind of danger.

It occurred to him that Sophy Woodruff might simply be what she looked—an innocent—then he dismissed it at once. Sir Frank's hunches were legendary. He wouldn't have been so rattled over a non-threat. And why would a young speech therapist in a children's clinic be tangled up with a cold-blooded bureaucrat like Elliott Fraser?

Unless Elliott was suffering his mid-life crisis. Connor shrugged cynically. Understandable, in Elliott's case, but what could be her excuse? Wouldn't there be plenty of virile lads her own age to appreciate her charms?

Strangely, instead of the boredom he'd expected, he felt intrigued enough to find out.

Surveillance wasn't his favourite activity, but he was as skilled as the best at the essential basic levels of tradecraft. His ability to blend into any crowd, or vanish in an instant, had saved his life, as well as others, from more than one assassin. If there was anything to uncover, he had absolute confidence he could do it, silently and undetectably, without a whisper of him ever having been there.

His blood quickened. Keeping an eye on her would be too easy, hardly work at all. He could still find time to catch up with his reading and keep the lines of contact open with his department on the other side of the world.

And he'd find that letter first.

CHAPTER FOUR

'SOPHY?'

Her grip tightened on her office phone. 'Oh. Oh, Elliott, I've been intending to call you. There's something—'

The curt, dry tones cut her off. 'I haven't time to chat. Look, er…now that we have something concrete to go on, I think we need to—discuss our situation.' The words were crisp and impersonal. 'Might as well get it out of the way. Dinner tomorrow evening a possibility for you?'

Her hopes leaped up. 'Oh.' Dinner…at his *home*? Visions of meeting Matthew and Elliott's wife opened out a golden vista of more dinners, family occasions, outings… 'That would be just—just *lovely*, Elliott. I'm so looking—'

'Good. The reservation's at The Sands. You know Shellwater?'

Her heart slumped back down. A hotel. Not exactly a welcome-daughter-into-my-life gesture. Still, it was dinner. An entire meal with the chance of real conversation, not a hasty coffee in some obscure café. She was making progress.

There was still hope. There was always hope.

'Meet you at seven.' He disconnected before she could say anything to warn him about her copy of the report. At least no one had approached him with it yet, perhaps because he'd been out of town. If Connor O'Brien planned to do something with it… Her insides clenched. If she couldn't get it back before she met Elliott, she'd have to confess to letting him down.

Although, she had to acknowledge her chances of retrieving it now had sunk to levels around the zero mark. She flinched from the notion of any further attempts at breaking in. Not that it would even be possible. To her mingled shame and amusement she'd noticed a locksmith at Connor's door the very same afternoon of the kiss. Locking her out.

Over the last week she'd encountered Connor several times in the gallery. The first time, the morning after the kiss, she'd been saying goodbye to one of her families at the top of the stairs. She'd been bending to talk to the child when she'd looked up to see *him* in his dark elegant suit, briefcase in hand, in the act of unlocking his door. He'd paused to watch the small transaction with his dark, unreadable gaze. As her eyes had met his, some electric frisson had crossed the space between them and she'd felt that hot, suffocating rush in her veins.

A couple of times he'd passed her, on the stairs or coming out of the coffee shop in the basement. Once he'd said, 'They're like the sky today.' Other times she'd tense as he approached, prepared for some mocking assault, but just like any ordinary acquaintance he'd say easily, 'Hello, Sophy.'

Except he wasn't ordinary. Every time she saw him it was a shock, and her pulse went into a dizzy race. He disturbed her dreams, and threw her senses into disarray. And she'd started imagining things. A couple of times, walking in the street, or queuing for the ferry turnstile at Circular Quay, she'd found herself looking around, unconsciously seeking his tall figure.

Even in the clinic, she couldn't ignore him. Cindy and the other receptionist had noticed him, and were always talking about him, relating sightings, *drooling*. Of course, they'd never had the experience of kissing him. They were lucky.

'Guess what, guess what? I asked him and he isn't married,' she heard Cindy screeching on one occasion. No need for Sophy to ask who she was on about. Who'd ever dream of asking him a question like that?

Sophy tried to close her ears to their fantasising, but it never worked. Like an addict, she found herself listening for news of him. She was ashamed to admit she'd even searched for him on the Internet, but hadn't found his name in particular, though there had been pages of references to some old Australian billionaire with the same surname who'd died the previous year and must have been a great benefactor, since he'd donated a whole wing to the Royal Children's Hospital.

That passport had been intriguing. According to the government Web site, the fact that it was red rather than the same blue as everyone else's meant he was a diplomat, or at least that he worked in foreign affairs or in some foreign embassy.

From what she'd glimpsed in her quick flip through, he'd certainly done a lot of travelling. She'd always pictured diplomats as being ultra smooth, sophisticated people with excellent manners and social savoir faire. She couldn't really imagine Connor O'Brien flattering women at embassy receptions, rushing to get them drinks or charming them on the dance floor. He was much more likely to be scowling at them from the sidelines. Unless…unless he was outside with them in the shrubbery. Kissing them.

But what was he doing in the Alexandra?

After Elliott's phone call she couldn't wait for her lunch hour so she could escape to the Gardens to think. As soon as she'd waved off the last of her morning clients, she threw her sandwich and a book into her bag, took the lifts down to the ground and braved the midday heat.

It was another scorcher. She stepped from the relative cool of the Alexandra straight into the merciless blaze of the sun. Heat rose from the pavement in a wave. As she waited for a break in the traffic the soles of her feet nearly fried inside her shoes, and she began to regret her impulse. Quite often friends from the Alexandra accompanied her to congregate under the trees, but today they'd had the good sense to shelter inside.

Still, the moment she passed through the iron gates and plunged into the labyrinth of shady avenues she felt the cooler air on her face and the deep, almost mystical feeling of peace green places inspired in her.

The usual lunchtime workers lazing on the grass were few and far between, preferring their air-conditioned offices. A couple of patient mothers stood wilting by the ponds as their children threw crumbs to the ducks, but Sophy bypassed the popular spots to walk further, beyond the rotunda and the central café to quieter regions, where the greenery was dense and lush. She chose a narrow, twisted path through the rainforest, paved with the rich, loamy leaf-fall from overhanging branches twisted with vines. The earthy scents of mulch and vegetation mouldered in the shimmering heat. The forest opened to a lawn where willows cast a deep shade, sweeping the grass with their long, graceful boughs, their luxuriant midsummer foliage shivering and trembling with every breath of air.

She sank onto the grass, then moved further in under the canopy to lean back against the trunk and dream in the aromatic, willow-scented air, her book face down on her lap, long leafy wands drifting around her. She imagined herself going to Elliott's house, feeling familiar there, being welcomed by his family and friends, treated like a daughter, a sister…

A tiny, niggling worry she'd been holding at bay forced its way forward.

Maybe she should cut those dreams off. Her own experience suggested that real life didn't necessarily work that way. People couldn't become like family unless they'd been raised as family. Unless… Really, perhaps she should face it. Unless they *were* family. Despite the kindness of her adoptive parents, they must have felt a barrier.

It was all about the bonding, Millie always said. Sophy had bonded with Henry and Bea, but they hadn't bonded with her. She didn't want to be ungrateful, but sometimes she wondered… Would they have just moved away and left her if she'd been their real daughter?

She'd wanted to go with them when she'd come to realise they were staying on with Lauren, but Bea had talked her into remaining behind to finish her uni course. Since she'd been well into her second year by then, and her clinical hospital practice had been organised, she'd seen the force of Bea's arguments, and stayed.

By the time the four years were up and she'd received her excellent job offer at the Alexandra, the urgency to follow them had diminished.

They'd paid her fare to fly over there for a visit once, and it had been fabulous, though too short. They wrote often, phoned at Christmas and on her birthday, and she'd been saving to fly over to see them again in her next holidays, but she still couldn't seem to get over the hole they'd left in her life.

Surely children were precious. She couldn't imagine abandoning a daughter if she had one. Giving away a child.

She let her mind drift, and as usual ended up dwelling on Connor O'Brien.

What did he hope to gain? Was it something she'd said that day in the mothers' room that had made him want to taunt her? Almost as though it had been mental telepathy, a movement made her glance up, and her heart skidded to a halt to see him standing there outside the tree's canopy, his dark eyes intent on her with that unfathomable expression.

It was such a shock she froze momentarily, hoping the wild fluttering inside her didn't show.

He was wearing casual trousers and a white, open-necked shirt, and carried a bag from the university bookshop.

'So this is where you hide yourself,' he murmured. 'I wondered.' He ducked under the hanging foliage and stepped into the shelter of the canopy, dropping onto the grass a metre or so away from her.

Her heart thudded into the mad erratic rhythm he always provoked, but she managed to say coolly enough, 'Doesn't seem to have worked, does it?'

Still, his words had pinged straight to her weakness. He *wondered* about her. Did that mean she was as vivid in his imagination as he was in hers? But he was an experienced man, sophisticated in the art of kissing. He would hardly have given her another thought, not in that way, anyway. Although why he had any interest in her at all was a mystery. Then she remembered the way he'd looked at her in the gallery, and felt the warm surge to her breasts, the shortening of her breath.

He rolled back his sleeves. She tried not to watch, but the exposure of his forearms, their scattering of black hairs, was a reminder of the glimpse she'd caught of his naked chest at their first encounter. She felt scorchingly aware of every small thing about him, the crisp black hair crinkling slightly at his temples, his lean, elegant hands, their nails clean and manicured.

He lounged back, one arm resting on his bent knee. Her eyes were drawn to a faint mist of moisture gathered in the bronzed hollow at the base of his throat. *Salt to taste.*

His dark gaze rested on her face with sensual appreciation. 'They're the colour of the sea today. Cool and deep and mysterious.' He drawled the words to give them added impact.

Mysterious. Thank heavens for that at least, though she didn't feel very mysterious. She felt—bombarded. That sexy note in his voice. He was being definitely flirty. No, bolder than flirty. Seductive.

She raised a cool, mysterious eyebrow. 'So what's a diplomat doing in the Alexandra?'

He answered at once in his deep, smooth tones. 'Ah, well, I'm not strictly a diplomat. Not what you'd call a career diplomat, anyway. I'm a lawyer. I was hired by the government as extra staff for the embassy in Iraq. My contract with them is finished, so I'm doing some reading to catch up on the domestic scene before I open my doors. Not that I would ever need to open them to you.'

She ignored the gibe. 'Why do they need a lawyer?'

He hesitated. 'They have quite a few lawyers in various departments. My field is humanitarian law. That means…well, in the international sense it deals mainly with the fallout of war. Prisoners, refugees, etc. Because of the war, the embassy in Baghdad has a heavy load of people requiring assistance. Some apply to come here as refugees, or Australians who get caught up in the war need advice.' He flashed her a mocking glance. 'I thought you'd have found some of this out when you were snooping.'

'Certainly it *looked* as if you were a lawyer.'

He didn't reply at once. She glanced at him and his acute dark eyes were fixed on her face, calculating, assessing her. Then he said with a quirk of his eyebrow, 'Only looked?'

She shrugged and plucked at a blade of grass. 'I'm not so sure you feel like one.'

He blinked, but his dark gaze didn't leave her face. 'To kiss, you mean?'

Her nerve jumped and she felt heat wash through her. She knew it showed in her face, but pride wouldn't let her lower her gaze. 'No,' she said, keeping her voice steady, conscious of her pulse beating in her temples. 'That's not what I mean.'

It was hard to appear cool when her heart felt as revved up as a Formula One racing engine. Her last words seemed to throb in a silence that stretched and stretched.

Connor, on the other hand, looked relaxed, his long limbs at ease. As though unaware of the tension, he said easily, 'What's that you're reading?'

She hesitated, then with the utmost reluctance flashed him the cover of her book, hoping he'd miss the couple engaged in the hot clinch. He screwed up his eyes and leaned forward to read the title aloud. 'What is it? A romance?'

'As a matter of fact.'

He smiled, as though to himself. As if he were amused by her choice, but accepted it as typical. 'Not my kind of thing.'

Unreasonably annoyed, she retorted, 'Maybe you should read some. You might learn how to treat a woman.'

He gave her a long look and the amusement in his eyes deepened. She felt her face grow hot and had to turn away to avoid that knowing, sinful scrutiny.

Oh, God, why had she said that? She knew now why he had that scar on his ribs. Other people besides herself wanted to kill him.

He plucked a willow frond from the tree and put the end between his lips. 'Found your letter?'

'You know I haven't.' There was a raw note in her voice.

'How would I know?'

'Because you have it.' She'd never meant to come straight out and accuse him, but the words slipped off her tongue before she could stop them.

He was silent. She could feel him choosing his words. 'Why do you think so? Why would I do something like that?'

'To torture me.' As soon as she'd said it, she flushed again, knowing how melodramatic it sounded.

She felt his eyes travel down her throat, to where her shirt opening hinted at the valley between her breasts. She lifted her gaze to his and recognised in his eyes' dark depths the desire that couldn't be concealed.

'Torture can be a two-way street,' he said softly.

She turned her face away and fought to calm her tumultuous pulse.

Connor noted the quick colour in her cheek and couldn't repress a small, dangerous surge of triumph. It was seductive to draw a response, and he instantly regretted the words. Temptation was always easier to fight unacknowledged.

'I told you the first time we met I haven't found your letter,' he said, to quell the vibrations he'd let loose. Anything to silence his conscience. He was rewarded to see hesitation in her face. To further convince her he added, 'If I had, I'd have given it to you. I have no interest in your correspondence.'

He felt unexpected remorse for having to deceive her. There was vulnerability in the creases of her smooth, pale forehead, but the truth was there was nothing he was more curious about now than the contents of that letter. Was it from a lover? Instructions from her controller? Although what situation would require the use of hard copies in these days of slick communication? He took in the soft flush of her cheeks, the rapid pulse in her throat, and his resistance to the idea of her being a player rose up again.

He couldn't imagine her as Elliott Fraser's mistress. His glance fell on the slim hand clutching the book in her lap. The nails were trimmed short, as if the hand was unafraid of dirt. Hardly the talons of a predator. Everything about her seemed—natural.

His palms tingled with an urgency to seize her slim, smooth arms, pull her across to him and taste her again. Her ripe mouth, the feel of her soft breasts. That delicious moment of her surrender had stayed with him. Remembering it now, he felt himself stir.

He made another attempt to initiate a peace move. 'Why do you think I have it? Was it because I—teased you the other morning?' He held out his hand to her. 'I shouldn't have. I'm sorry.'

She met his eyes with a clear intelligence in her blue gaze that shook him. Her voice was low and earnest. 'Whatever you say…whatever you *say* your intentions are—I *know*, I have a very strong feeling that you're lying to me.'

Stunned, he failed to react at first when she stood up and snatched up her book and bag. Then he wanted to grab her hand and pull her back down beside him, convince her he meant well. Kiss her. But she flung through the screen of willow fronds and walked quickly away, almost at a run.

His muscles tensed in the almost irresistible male compulsion to pursue her, sweet-talk her, force her to acknowledge the attraction, but he knew he must restrain the urge. Once desire had been spoken of, sooner or later consummation would follow, then all the in-evitable madness—passion, addiction, obsession…

The *hell* when he had to leave her.

He shouldn't have succumbed to the temptation today to hear her voice. Already he'd allowed his discipline to slip, and now he'd be haunted by the vision of her dreaming here under the willow tree.

With an effort he forced himself to concentrate on the task in hand.

Though his surveillance had been necessarily limited without the benefit of back-up, he was pretty sure she hadn't met Elliott since Monday of last week. Her routine was fairly predictable, divided between the Alexandra and her home in Neutral Bay. No evening rendezvous to date. Apart from one evening playing netball at a local club with her friends, she seemed to spend a lot of her time in her garden greenhouse.

It was time to focus some attention on Elliott. Where did he go in the evenings?

CHAPTER FIVE

WHAT did a woman wear to dine with her father? Something modest, but elegant to show she thought him worth it. Pretty, so he could be proud of her.

Sophy had quite sickening butterflies, partly from excitement, and partly from dread at having to tell Elliott the truth about losing the letter. Nearly every piece of clothing she owned was strewn across the bed before she settled again on her initial choice, a slim dinner dress in purple silk georgette with narrow straps.

Demure enough, she hoped, even though the dress fell short of her knees, and cool, even for the heavy heat hanging over the city. The shade enhanced her eyes, and in the right light somehow managed to find violet highlights in her hair. She twisted the dark mass into a loose chignon and secured it with a tortoiseshell clasp.

Should she confess to him at once, she wondered, fastening in a dangly earring, or wait till the meal was under way and some genuine rapport had been established?

In the beginning she'd planned to drive there, but the possibility she'd be drinking wine decided her in the end on taking a taxi.

She left it late to phone for one, then had a nerve-racking wait while the minutes ticked closer to seven. Would Elliott still be there if she arrived late? He always seemed so pressed for time, so impatient to get away, her chances of getting to know him could be ruined by this one ridiculous hitch.

'Wow.' Zoe paused when she saw her, her green eyes widening. 'Hot date? Come on, Soph. Who is it? *Spill.*'

Normally she'd have told everything. So when she hedged with, 'Er…just meeting a friend,' her flatmate's curiosity shot up along with her eyebrows, but, without lying, it was the best she could do until Elliott gave her the all-clear. Then she'd happily shout her secret to the world.

The taxi came at last, too close on seven for comfort, and carried her through the dusk that was still warm, even for midsummer. As they turned into the Steyne and drove along the beachfront, the full moon had just announced itself on the south-eastern horizon, a soothing relief after the angry sun. The cab slowed, and they drove in under the portico of a large hotel with several balconied storeys.

The Sands.

Sophy paid the driver and got out. Even this close to the sea the air was unusually still and warm, but, after the searing heat of the day, comfortable on her skin. She took a moment to smooth her dress with her palms while she surveyed the hotel entrance, her pulse ticking along too fast, every nerve and instinct on edge.

At one end of the hotel, tables and chairs spilled onto a terrace strung with coloured lights, and she could hear what sounded like the hum of a crowded bar. A flickering neon sign announced a casino as part of the complex's attractions. It was a resort, and she felt some surprise. She'd never have imagined Elliott dining in a place like this.

Inside, there was an excited buzz to the busy lobby as people came and went to the various entertainments. A careful scan showed no sign of Elliott among the patrons seated in the lounges. From somewhere came the strains of a band and occasional applause, while through an archway a wide bar thronged with the noisy pre-dinner crowd. Beside it, separated by a barrier of palms and cycads, was the hotel restaurant, already filling with diners.

She approached the entrance and looked eagerly for Elliott. The large room was inviting, all gleaming wood surfaces, with candles on the tables catching the sparkle of crystal and cutlery. Down a step, a lower level opened to the beach terrace, where a tiny dance floor had been laid under the lights.

There was an energy to the place, and she felt a surge of pleasant anticipation. Had he chosen it to please her?

This was it, she thought. Make or break time with her father. Conscious of her thudding heart, she was about to take her turn at the desk and give Elliott's name to the head waiter when Elliott materialised beside her.

'Miss Woodruff is my guest,' he cut in before she could say anything.

There was a moment of awkwardness when she half expected him to kiss her cheek, but it didn't quite come off, though he greeted her with courtesy. She held out her hand but he seemed not to notice. He must be nervous, too, she thought, curling up her fingers, though she suffered a faint twinge of anxiety. Still, realistically, how could he be expected to know how to behave with a new daughter?

They'd work it out, she told herself. It would come with time.

'This way,' he said smoothly, almost touching her arm, but not quite, as he indicated a table on the upper level by the bar.

She smiled her thanks as the waiter pulled out her chair, and placed the linen napkin on her lap. While Elliott made bland conversation, about the heat, Sydney traffic, she kept smiling her responses, barely able to speak for trying to control a sudden, irresistible wave of emotion pricking at the backs of her eyes. To think she was actually dining with her father.

The menus were presented, and she read hers through a mist. She hardly knew what she ordered. But Elliott's discussion with the waiter about the wine gave her a chance to recover some poise. She listened with pleasure, though she wasn't surprised he was so knowledgeable. Everything about him, his articulate command of language, his clothes and grooming, suggested he was an experienced man of the world.

It wasn't her first meeting with him, but the previous ones had been rushed and rather furtive, in places with poor lighting. He'd seemed stressed and curt on those occasions. Now he was more relaxed, and while they conversed she had a better opportunity to study him, and see him for the person he truly was.

His hair had nearly all turned to silver, though there were still dark edges at the temples. His face was well-shaped, with regular features. His grey eyes looked cold, but he almost certainly would have been a handsome man when he was young. It wasn't surprising that her mother had been attracted to him, even if they had only made love on the one occasion. Although Elliott claimed he'd hardly known her, it nagged at Sophy that he *had* known that she'd died. So he must still have known her to some degree, or known *of* her, despite the way he'd told it. And he must have known she'd had a child. She hadn't been adopted by the Woodruffs until she was two years old.

She thought she could understand him glossing over the truth a little. And with all the tremulous emotion churning around inside her she decided to hold off interrogating him. He was probably just as much an emotional melting pot tonight as she was herself. He wouldn't have invited her here if he didn't intend for their relationship to develop. There was no use spoiling things.

The chardonnay arrived and was poured, the menus were removed and a small silence fell. Elliott Fraser sat with downcast eyes, taking a moment to gather his words. Then he said very quietly, 'I'm prepared to give you a cash payment of one hundred thousand dollars, once and once only. That's quite a sum for a young woman like yourself. In return, I expect you to sign a confidentiality agreement. My lawyers are drawing it up.'

The words broke through her blur as if from a very long distance.

She stared at him, uncomprehending, then leaned forward. Her lips felt suddenly numb. 'Do you think I want money?'

He studied her, frowning, a hard light in his eyes. 'Well, what do you want, Sophy? Why does an adult woman hunt down a man she has no connection with, apart from a mere technicality—an accident of birth?'

After a moment of shocked paralysis she shook her head. 'Oh. No, no. That's not—that's not it at all. Please…' Impulsively, she reached across and touched his hand, but he drew it away at once as if he'd been touched by a leper. Something like a knife stabbed her insides. In her dismay her throat became as hoarse as a dry gulch. 'I…I only wanted to—'

'To what?'

The ridiculousness of her hopes flashed in on her and her words dried up. As she faced the hostile reality of him an excruciating embarrassment invaded her. What a fool she'd been. As far as he was concerned she was a stranger. An accident of birth.

She mumbled, 'To—to get to know you.' She felt the heat crawl up from her ankles and creep to the roots of her hair. How dumb she must sound. If he ever had any inkling of the dreams she'd allowed to grow…

His mobile phone rang, and, still frowning at her, he took it out and spoke into it. He rose, the phone to his ear, and murmured, 'I must take this call. Excuse me, I'll be back in a minute.' He hesitated. 'We'll…er…talk.' Then he walked away, talking into his phone.

She clung to her chair, every muscle in her body clenched. A wave of nausea washed through her. Who'd have thought her evening would have ended so bitterly?

She felt an urgent need to get away. Find a cab, fly home and hide herself. Forget Elliott Fraser and the whole damn thing. It wasn't as if she needed a father figure in her life, was it? She already had one she loved quite extremely. At the thought of Henry her eyes filled up with tears. She wasn't sure she ever could bear to lay eyes on Elliott again.

Except…she wasn't a child, or a *nothing*. The pleasant, busy restaurant swam and she tried to will the tears away for fear of someone at a neighbouring table noticing her dabbing at her eyes. So what if she was the result of an accident? She was still a person. She had a heart and feelings, hopes and aspirations, affections, talents… Her fingernails dug into her palms.

She couldn't allow herself to be so dismissed without standing up for herself. She'd started the process, for whatever insane reason. It had seemed like the right thing, the *human* thing to do, almost like a sign from Fate the day she'd first seen him in the clinic. Other people sought their birth parents without this sort of reception.

Her disappointment turned to dismay on Elliott's account. What did his response show about him?

She must at least finish the evening with dignity. Make him understand that not everyone was eager to use their biological connections for financial gain. Although, a man who thought that way… Would it ever be possible to convince him?

The waiter brought the first courses, and her soup sat cooling in front of her. As often lately when she was alone, she had that strange sensation in the nape of her neck, as if she were being watched. She glanced around at the other diners, but they seemed blissfully unaware of her and her little problems. They were tucking into their food, chatting and laughing, at ease with themselves and the world. None of them looked to be suffering a crisis. Life was going on for people with normal family connections.

After a while the waiter appeared and suggested removing the meals, to keep warm until Elliott returned.

The call was taking some time.

It was none of his affair, Connor thought, hunching forward on his bar-stool. Sophy Woodruff wasn't his responsibility. If he leaned a little to the left of the shrubbery, he could see her quite clearly, reflected in the mirror behind the bar. She was sitting quite straight, a stiffness in her posture, like pride. Or hurt.

He glanced at his watch. Elliott had been gone nearly ten minutes. He realised he should have been more alert to Elliott's departure from his table. Though, surely he wouldn't have walked out on her? If they were lovers...

They couldn't be lovers. Where had been the touches, the lingering glances?

He considered the moment when she'd leaned towards Elliott. There'd been supplication in the gesture, pleading... Elliott was a chilly guy, by anyone's standards, but his response had been curious, to say the least. What man in his right mind would have resisted her?

Although, whatever had taken place between them in that tense little confrontation hadn't looked like a lovers' quarrel. Where was the fire and passion? He remembered enough about intimacy with a woman to recognise when it was missing. So how far had the affair gone? Had they slept together more than once?

Still, it did have all the hallmarks. The meetings, the place. He glanced about him at the mix of dress worn by the clientele. As if on cue an Elvis impersonator entertaining the crowd in the neighbouring bar smooged into 'Love Me Tender'. No fear of Elliott running into his acquaintances here.

An unpleasant thought assailed him. Surely she wasn't part-timing as an escort?

The bartender cocked an eye at him but Connor shook his head. His drink could last all night if necessary. As he could, occupying his corner with the chameleon skill he'd honed to a fine art.

He glanced at the bar clock. Thirteen minutes. Where the hell was Elliott? Was he imagining it, or was there desperation in the look Sophy Woodruff was casting about her? Was she starting to worry about her rich Romeo?

Not that it mattered to Connor O'Brien. He just wished he hadn't been cursed with this vivid imagination. He was only guessing she was distressed from the tension in her slender frame. So what if Fraser had hurt her? She'd learn from it and maybe steer clear of married, older guys in future.

Although he needed to be realistic. Why would a young woman

want a middle-aged man like Elliott, when she'd almost certainly have hot-blooded, younger guys lining up for a taste of those luscious lips, her warm, vibrant body, so soft and pliant to the touch—unless it had to do with the Fraser millions?

His musings about Elliott's age and virility suggested another possibility for his lengthening absence. Maybe the guy had some health problem. Connor got casually off the bar-stool and strolled around the corner to the men's room. There were a few men in there, but no Elliott. He walked out again to survey the lobby. The crowd was beginning to quieten, but he could see no sign of the ageing silvertail. He turned down the corridor to the car-park entrance and peered through the glass doors.

His car was still where he'd left it, parked a few spaces along from Elliott's. At least, from the space where Elliott's *had* been.

The rat had run.

He felt a dangerous quickening in his pulse as he strode back to his corner of the bar. He tried to cool it with an astringent dose of professional realism. Either she was a gold-digger, or she was infatuated with an older man, neither prospect very desirable.

So why did he so desire?

He shouldn't go over there. Revealing his presence would be a mistake. It would jeopardise his investigation. He didn't know enough yet to exonerate her from having a hostile agenda, did he? And she wasn't a fool. She wouldn't swallow the coincidence of his being at the same hotel on the same night.

Unless he could come up with a story.

Another glance in the mirror. He saw her look bravely about her, a bright little expectant smile on her lips, as if to signal to the world that her date would be back at any second, and his grip tightened on his glass.

The bastard, leaving her alone in a place like this, a plum ripe for the plucking to every sleazy opportunist.

God, he was playing with fire, and he knew it. She was a walking, breathing, flesh-and-blood temptation, a bigger threat to him than a dark alleyway and a sly stiletto blade.

His struggle intensified. He couldn't afford any involvements. Although if he just talked to her, maybe she'd give him a simple explanation for her association with Elliott. A little conversation could do no harm. It didn't have to lead to a night of passion.

Not unless…she wanted it to.

His brain filled with images of soft, firm flesh, slender, shapely limbs tangled with his among the sheets, but he pushed them aside. She wasn't the type.

He lifted his glass to his lips and drained it. Suddenly the hunch he'd had about her overwhelmed him with rock-solid certainty. She was no agent for any intelligence service. She was a speech therapist in a children's clinic.

Looking to improve her financial status with an older, married man, perhaps. Way out of her depth, undoubtedly.

But that was *all*.

'Sorry, I have an emergency I must deal with. Please continue your dinner as my guest. I'll be in touch. E. Fraser.'

Sophy crumpled the page of hotel stationery in her hand. The rejection slammed in deeper. She could hardly have expected Dad, but *E. Fraser*?

A band had set up down on the lower level, and a few people were gyrating about on the dance floor to an old Stones song. She could feel some nearby couples' curious glances at her as they speculated about Elliott's desertion.

She gathered up her purse to leave, then tensed in shock. The lean, athletic figure of Connor O'Brien was strolling through the dining-room entrance, with all the casual assurance of someone for whom The Sands was a second home.

Her pulse plunged into a wild racket, fuelled by a sure, instinctive knowledge. He was here, because *she* was.

He was following her.

She saw him lower his dark head to speak to the head waiter, then glance straight across at her. Tensing, she reached for the wine specials pamphlet tucked between the salt and pepper shakers and pretended to read, refusing to look up, as if the specials were of more importance than the missing fragments of the Dead Sea Scrolls. All the time she knew Connor O'Brien was advancing on her with cool, steady purpose.

'Sophy.'

The quiet resonance of his deep voice had its usual volcanic effect on her insides. It took a moment before she could gather the emotional energy to raise her eyes from the pamphlet, and when she did, her lashes seemed to join in the wild fluttering of the rest of her. He was all in shades of black—black dinner suit, black shirt and gleaming black silk tie. With his ebony hair and eyebrows and midnight-dark eyes it was hardly safe to look at him, he was so tall and lean and sinfully handsome, looking down at her with that faintly amused glint as if he knew, he *knew*, damn him, how he affected her.

'This *is* a pleasant surprise.'

'For you, perhaps,' she said, finding her voice. Comprehension flickered in his dark gaze and she had the horrible suspicion she might have let him know just how humiliated she was to be sitting there alone.

'What are you doing here?' As if she didn't know.

He glanced about, as if in search of her companions. 'Mind if I sit down?' He pulled out Elliott's chair, and dropped into it before she could protest. 'I was supposed to meet someone, but I'm embarrassed to say she stood me up.'

A jagged sensation assailed her in the midst of all her chaos. Who was this woman Connor O'Brien had wanted to meet? 'I can understand your feeling embarrassed,' she said softly. 'As I can understand her wanting to stand you up.'

A muscle moved at the corner of his mouth. 'It's not something I'm accustomed to. I must be losing my touch.'

'Your touch isn't so fantastic, if you want to know.'

Their eyes met and he smiled. Sophy felt the flush rise in her cheeks as the memory of her enthusiastic participation in that kiss shimmered in the air between them. She lowered her lashes, determined not to let his sexy, teasing gaze get to her, although her pulse had started a mad, erratic gallop. Her suspicion that he'd followed her grew even stronger. It was impossible to imagine a woman standing him up.

'What about you?' His voice was as smooth as silk. 'Are you with someone?'

'Of course. Well, I—*was* with—someone. My—friend was called away to an emergency.'

His eyebrows lifted. 'Pity. And he didn't take you with him?'

'No. Well, he—he couldn't.'

'Ah.' He took the chardonnay Elliott had ordered from the ice bucket and examined the label before putting it back. 'He must be crazy.'

She glanced quickly at him, but his dark eyes were warm, without the usual mockery that threw her so off balance. For a second she nearly gave him the benefit of the doubt, until he had to ruin it.

'He wasn't that silver-haired guy you were with just now, was he? Don't you think he's a bit old for you? He's probably past it. He saw you sitting here like a ripe little peach in the candlelight and realised he wasn't up to it, so he scampered.'

She drew a sharp breath, then leaned forward and hissed, 'I knew it. You've been spying on me, haven't you? Just what's your game, Connor O'Brien? Why are you stalking me?'

Something like shock flickered in his dark irises and a muscle twinged in his lean, bronzed cheek. '*Stalking* you?'

She was sorry she'd blurted it out like that, because he stiffened and his expression grew quite haughty and defensive, as if she'd insulted his very honour. With his high, austere cheekbones, his dark brows and lashes, he looked so stern, such a model of outraged decency, she wondered if she'd been imagining things again and overreacting.

With cool deliberation he poured a little of the chardonnay into Elliott's glass, swirled it about, inhaled its scent, then tasted it. 'I was here before you, as it happens,' he said. 'I was waiting in the bar, when who should come sashaying up to the restaurant but Sophy Woodruff? How do I know *you* aren't stalking *me*?'

'Oh. You know I'm not.'

'How do I know? You break into my office—'

'You *know* why I did that.'

'Oh, that's right,' he said, looking sardonic. 'You came to apologise. You wanted to kiss and make up.'

She gasped. 'Rubbish. I only kissed you that time because—I was—*desperate*.'

He laughed and she could have bitten off her tongue. *God*. Why did he always have to trick her into saying things that sounded so green? He must have thought she was the most naive and unsophisticated woman he'd ever met.

He plucked the wine specials pamphlet from her nerveless fingers and gave it a cursory glance. 'Fascinating ,' he murmured. 'I can see why you were so interested.'

The impulsive words burst from her. 'I really loathe you, Connor O'Brien.'

His eyes lifted to hers and she saw their amusement gleam with a sexual challenge that pierced through her flimsy defences like a sword through paper.

'Are you sure?' he said softly.

He wasn't joking now. She shook her head, scrabbling for some words to come up with a massive and convincing denial, but he forestalled her.

'Shh. Don't say anything you might regret. I'm sorry, all right? Truly. For everything.' With rueful charm he placed his hand over his heart, or at the least the place where it ought to have been. 'Isn't it time we let bygones be bygones? Come on, you know you want to.'

Then he smiled. He never really had before, not like that, though she'd noticed his eyes smile, or soften. Now, as his lean, handsome face illuminated with warmth, the breath nearly seized in her lungs and her interior melted like honey dripping through the comb.

Ravished to their entrails, all of her instincts made a wild, excited surge towards *'Yes.'* Well, nearly all. There was still that nebulous part of her that found something worrying about him, even though he was so straight and tall and gorgeous.

On the other hand, he had an honourable profession most people, including herself, found impressive. Zoe seemed agog to hear more about him every night.

It was hard to know how to trust him, he was so difficult to talk to, with his mockery and sardonic teasing. There were barriers around him she had no idea how to breach. And, of course, there was her letter.

Although in truth, after that day in the Gardens, she'd actually started to believe in his innocence about that. It just didn't make sense that a human rights lawyer would steal a stranger's DNA profile just for the hell of it. She'd even started to go soft on him in some of her other imaginings.

And right now he seemed sincere. The dark eyes dwelling on her face were intent, and so attractive, with golden shards of candlelight reflected in their depths.

She didn't want to give in too easily, though. She said stiffly, 'You'd have to change your attitude.'

His black brows twitched. 'What attitude?'

'You know very well. Always mocking people.'

'Oh, that. All right. I promise I won't mock. So...' He smiled and held out his hand. 'Friends?'

Somehow, despite the constriction of her lungs brought about by being dazzled by smiling dark eyes, she managed to breathe, 'I suppose. Friends.'

She allowed him to take her hand into his smooth, warm clasp. The glow in his dark eyes intensified, and it took him several vibrant seconds to let her hand go. When she got it back, it was still madly zinging.

'I like your hair up,' he said warmly. 'It makes me want to pull it all down.'

Did friends say things like that? Perhaps it was the aftermath of emotional upheaval, after her rocky start to the evening, but there was a dizzy, racing sensation in her blood.

She tried not to show it with a cool demeanour. 'Oh. Well, anyway, I'm about to go home now, so—'

He trapped her hand again. 'No, don't go.' He signalled a passing waiter and the boy changed direction and swerved their way at once. 'A menu, please. Miss Woodruff will dine with me. Won't you, Sophy?'

Perhaps she should have refused, but time was marching on, and what with all she'd been through, with Elliott leaving her to rot in a public place miles away from anywhere, she still hadn't managed even a bite to eat. It couldn't count as a date, exactly, but she'd hardly be human not to have felt the tiniest twinge of pleasure and pride to have such a prime example of tall, sexy masculinity looking at her like that.

'And we'd like one of those tables down there,' Connor informed the waiter, indicating the terrace. 'Wouldn't we, Sophy?' He bathed her again in one of those intimate, seductive glances and her bones melted.

Those tables did look inviting. The musicians had started an old Bee Gees number, and couples were swarming to dance under the coloured lights. While the waiter transferred their setting and darted away to find him a menu, Connor held out his hand to her and drew her down to the lower level and out to the terrace.

There was a magic in the vibrant midsummer night, or maybe it was the exhilaration of Connor's arm slipping around her waist. The warmer-than-usual air caressed her skin and made her feel pleasantly sensual. The moon had risen into its full glory, and hung seemingly quite close, the breathtaking golden orb glowing in silent mystery. There was the occasional white flash of a wave breaking on the sand, and always underlying the noise and activity of the restaurant the constant swoosh and fall, the rush of foam on the beach.

Connor saw Sophy Woodruff's lovely glowing face as she gazed at her surroundings and felt something inside him lurch. With an effort, he dragged his gaze back to the waiter and ordered the snapper. He wouldn't have risked it in some places, but he had complete confidence in Elliott's choice of restaurant. There was nothing wrong with his chardonnay selection, either, so he settled in to fill Elliott's shoes, drink his wine, eat his coquilles, woo his girl. It was, after all, a golden opportunity.

He'd had a twinge of doubt earlier, but seeing her now enjoying her tempura mushrooms, dipping them into their sauce with such naturalness and poise, he allowed himself to relax. He reminded himself that if she were Elliott's girlfriend, however soft she looked, she was no ingénue, likely to pin too much on a casual evening.

And she did look luscious, the lavender of her dress reflected in her eyes, her smooth, bare arms and shoulders meltingly soft in the candlelight. The soft fabric of her bodice made two graceful curves over the creamy swells of her breasts and dipped to the shadowy valley in between. His lips tingled at the thought of tracing those delicious curves, but he quelled the image.

This was work. There'd never be a better opportunity to broach the subject head on. Enough information tonight, and he could wrap it up and report back to Sir Frank.

He kept the conversation firmly on her, finding out what he could about the women she lived with, her schooling, her parents in England. Much of it coincided with what he'd already found out himself.

She seemed so frank and open, if she *were* acting and it was all a cover, she was good. But could she be? His doubts returned every time he met her clear gaze.

He had to know. It could risk the rapport he was building, but he had to find out, once and for all. He chose his moment when they were nearly through their main courses.

'There was something very familiar about your friend,' he said casually. 'He's not Elliott Fraser by any chance, is he?'

Her eyes flew to his. The slim hands wielding the salad servers jerked and remained poised in the air for a second.

'Do you know him?'

'Not exactly. But my father and his were great friends. They were in business together at one time.'

'No, really? Goodness, that's such a coincidence.' Sophy stared at him, trying to accommodate the notion of him knowing Elliott and his family, however remotely. What were the odds? she wondered, examining the likelihood from all sides. She shook her head. 'It's quite amazing.'

'Not really.' He gave an easy shrug. 'Not if you know anything about the old Sydney establishment. All those old boys know each other, join the same clubs, go to the same concerts, send their kids to the same schools. Dad played golf with Sir Frank every Thursday for thirty years. You've heard of Sir Frank Fraser?'

'No,' she heard herself say, raising her glass to her suddenly dry lips. 'Elliott hasn't mentioned him.'

'Oh. So—you and Elliott haven't known each other very long?'

She lowered her gaze, reluctant to be reminded of her disappointment. There was a painful raw spot inside her now with Elliott's name on it. Just thinking about him hurt. Still, she couldn't repress the craving for more information. After all, this was her *grandfather* Connor was talking about.

She sent him an oblique glance. 'No, we haven't.'

He was silent, a small frown creasing his brow.

'What's the matter?' she enquired.

'Just that…' He narrowed his gaze and hesitated, as though seeking a way into a difficult subject. Then he shrugged. 'I guess—Fraser may not have told you he has a wife.'

She looked sharply at him. His eyes were watchful on her face. Surely he didn't really think…

'Are you serious?' She might almost have laughed if the implications hadn't been so insulting. Her Lana Turner impersonation must have been better than she'd thought. She leaned forward, demanding, 'Do you honestly think I'm having an *affair* with Elliott?'

He paused in the act of pouring wine into her glass. 'Well, you tell me.'

She stared at him in amazement. People swayed to the music, lovers were whispering under the moon, but Connor O'Brien was gazing intently at her with a grim expression, waiting to hear what excuse she had about seeing a married man.

'Well, apart from the fact that he's—' She pulled herself up just in time. She'd come too close then to blurting out the truth. Without lying, though, it was hard to know what to say, or how much. She didn't want to risk alienating him and wrecking the new accord. Hedging, she said flirtily, 'Why should I tell you?'

He dropped his dark lashes for an instant, then said softly, 'Because I need to know.'

The words thrilled through her like a wave. Perhaps it *was* a date. Another realisation sprang to the forefront of her mind. If he'd truly suspected, even for a second, that she was seeing Elliott, then he mustn't have read her letter. He couldn't have stolen it. He'd been speaking the sincere truth.

As she contemplated his lean, strong face across the table her heart swelled with a joyous relief. She could acquit him.

A whole new world of possibilities opened up before her. She could trust him, they were friends now, he *liked* her… More than liked, judging by that hot little flame in the eyes flickering to her throat and breasts, rousing sparks in her blood and sending her pulse into a giddy race. Compared to him, the boys she'd known before had been just that. Boys.

She raised the last forkful of filet and salad to her lips and said carefully, 'Actually, Elliott did tell me he has a wife.'

'And a child?' he added, suddenly quite still.

She nodded. 'Yes. I saw Matthew—his little boy. He brought him to the clinic.'

He set down his knife and fork. 'Is that where you met Fraser? At the clinic?' There was a note of incredulity in his voice.

She hesitated, uneasily aware that if she made it sound too mysterious, she'd only fuel his curiosity. 'That's where I first saw him. I only met him later. There was something I needed to—speak with him about.'

'Oh.' His eyes lit up. 'So the boy's your client?'

That excuse would have been convenient, but regretfully she had to wave it goodbye. 'Well, no.'

It would have looked curious, she supposed, observing Connor's bemused gaze. She wished she could just be honest and tell the truth, but despite Elliott's treatment of her this evening, it would be such a betrayal. He might not want a daughter, but without her knowing the consequences he was so fearful of, how could she judge him?

With a little shake of his head Connor O'Brien complained, 'You're being very mysterious.'

'I know, I know. I don't mean to be. It's just that—I have an agreement. I've made a promise, and I must keep it.'

'Oh, a promise.' He nodded, his eyes narrowed. 'Right.'

Instead of being satisfied, though, he only looked more puzzled than ever. His black brows edged closer together. 'You're not in any trouble, are you, Sophy?' He spoke lightly, as though teasing, but the dark eyes on her face were keen. Surprisingly—though it might have been a trick of the candlelight—they seemed touched with concern.

'No, of course not. What do you mean, *trouble*? Just because I met a man for dinner?'

He sat back, contemplating her, his lean fingers toying with the stem of his glass. 'An older, married man. *Much* older, and much married, in fact.' He raised his glass to his lips and said meditatively, 'He'll be keen to make amends, I guess. I'm betting tomorrow he'll send you flowers, at least. Maybe chocolates. Who knows? He might even pitch for diamonds.'

'Diamonds. Oh, please. Get real.'

'Well, he *is* very wealthy.'

'*Is* he?' Her eyes widened involuntarily. She had assumed her father was quite well off, judging by his clothes and the fact that he looked like a successful businessman, but this made it seem as if he might be very well off indeed.

Her heart sank and she chewed her lip. It wasn't good news for her. If Elliott was rich and powerful, he probably had a lot more to lose by acknowledging a twenty-three-year-old daughter. Perhaps she should have found out more about him before jumping in feet first. She had looked for information about him on the Internet, of course, several times since she was eighteen, without finding him mentioned anywhere. He wasn't listed in any phone book. She'd had to rely on what he'd acknowledged about himself.

Import-export, was what he'd told her at that initial meeting. What did that mean? Probably just a smokescreen to hold her at bay. Like inviting her here tonight, then walking out on her because he thought she was an opportunist.

Diamonds indeed. What a laugh.

Then the full horrific implication of Connor O'Brien's meaning finally seeped through. Did he think she was a—*prostitute*?

Unfortunately, the insult came too close on the heels of the wound Elliott had inflicted. She met his gaze angrily. 'Oh, I get it. Thanks. It's good to know people think the best of you.'

To her absolute shame then, some emotional subterranean river chose that instant to rise to the surface and attempt to flood its banks. Tears sprang into her eyes and she had to turn her face away. She tried to smile and say something offhand, but her croaky voice was a dead giveaway.

How many magazine articles had she read that stipulated that whatever a woman did, on no account should she weep in front of a man? Especially one giving her a candlelit dinner. Her housemates would have been appalled at her letting down the side so disgracefully. Men only felt contempt for women who used tears. She hated them quite heartily herself. If there'd been any members of the Avengers netball team present, she wouldn't have blamed them if they'd stormed across the room, grabbed her by the throat and shaken her till her brainbox rattled.

In Connor O'Brien's case, there was a sudden rigidity in his posture. His fingers seemed to freeze to his glass. As she fought to regain control his stunned dismay reached her from across the table. Even in her moments of extremis, she forgave him his blunder. After all, he wasn't to know what Elliott had said before he dumped her. She blinked rapidly a dozen or so times and somehow forced the dam back behind the wall.

He broke the fraught silence, treading gingerly. 'Er…you didn't know the Frasers were wealthy?'

The dam wall threatened to burst again, and she lifted her shoulders in stiff denial. 'Whatever Elliott Fraser *has*, whatever he *does*, is nothing to do with me.'

The lines of his lean, strong face tautened. 'Look, I…' He reached over and gently grasped her arm. Shamelessly, despite her turmoil, fireworks flared in her flesh. 'I'm sorry if I seemed to imply… I saw you there with him and…well, I was naturally intrigued.'

She glanced down at his hand on her arm, and he released her and sat back. It cost her a struggle, but she managed to keep her voice cool and steady. 'Maybe you're just naturally suspicious.'

He shrugged and his handsome face hardened into its usual calm expression, though there was a slight darkening of the taut skin across his cheekbones.

He kept glancing at her, and the silence grew alive with vibrations, as though her small upset had generated some massive, underground repercussion. Her fault, she castigated herself, for showing her true feelings over what had been perfectly natural questions anyone would have asked.

Their eyes clashed accidentally and the hunger in Connor O'Brien's clutched at her breath and made her insides curl up at the edges. She glanced quickly away, her body absolutely zinging with awareness, and tried to keep her attention on the dancers, though all the time she was conscious of him lounging back in his chair, his long fingers loose on the stem of his glass.

She felt a smouldering heat surge to her breasts. It was as clear as the moon sailing over the sea. He didn't trust her.

But he wanted her. Sensing it stirred something primitive in her blood.

Since the kiss—why couldn't she admit it?—she'd dreamed of him. Kissing him. Now that she'd had first-hand experience of how very sensuous his lips could be, looking at them made something coil deep in the pit of her abdomen.

She felt a trembling certainty about him. With his beautiful hands, his long, lean limbs, so much about him was so attractive.

The waiter came to remove the plates, then offered her the dessert menu. Connor O'Brien waved his away and ordered coffee. She opted for a slice of chocolate truffle cake.

All through the exchange with the waiter she could feel Connor's hot gaze devouring her like a dissatisfied wolf, his sexy mouth grim, the dark shadow of tomorrow's beard adding to the little frown lowering his black brows. Dying to know more, she supposed. Weighing up what sort of woman she was. *Judging* her.

He lowered his glance, but not before she saw his eyes. God, that hungry little flame made her feel reckless.

'Anyway,' she challenged on an impulse to inject some lightness into the mood, 'what's it to you, Connor? You aren't checking up on me, are you?'

Something flickered in his expression, but he said smoothly, 'Hardly.'

But he was mad keen to know about her, she could feel it in him. And she could sense the desire simmering in him, connecting him to her like a burning fuse. Whatever this was, it was for real, she realised with an adrenaline lurch. It was nothing like the tepid attractions she'd felt in the past. Even being grilled by him on such an uncomfortable subject somehow fanned the fever in her blood.

The slice of cake appeared before her, a faint dew on the frosting, scrolls of flaked chocolate on top. Beside it was a strawberry in a swirl of raspberry sauce.

'Well,' she said, taking up her fork, 'however it might look, you're mistaken. My—association with Elliott Fraser is not what you seem to think.'

He hardly seemed to be listening. His dark, sensual gaze was devouring her face, lingering on her mouth. 'What is it, then?'

She sat up straight, admonishing him with a stern look. 'It's a private matter between him and me, and no one else.' She waited for him to reply, and when he didn't felt herself flush with annoyance. 'Oh. Do I look so *hard* to you?'

Connor roused himself from his sensual contemplation of her. The sincerity in her wounded blue gaze struck deep. He took in the defiant tilt of her delicate chin, the poignant little hurt smile on her lips, and his suspicions fell in a heap.

After all the lies and deceits he'd lived through in the last few years, he should know truth when he heard it. He cursed himself for a fool. He'd been seeing her as a suspect, when the blindest idiot could see... Whatever the private matter was, she was an innocent. Sir Frank had got it wrong. A desirable, tantalising innocent.

'No.' He heard his own voice growl up from his depths. 'You don't look hard.'

She smiled at him then, with such sweet generosity he felt like the biggest bastard on the eastern seaboard. She waggled her fork at him and said huskily, 'That's just as well if we're going to be friends.'

He leaned back in his chair and watched her slide the fork through her truffle cake and lift it to her mouth. Each time her lips closed over a morsel he imagined the chocolate melting on her pink tongue, trails of it trickling off into the moist slipstream of her mouth. His loins stirred into dangerous life.

She picked up the strawberry in her slim fingers and bit into it.

He closed his eyes briefly, his body a torture chamber. Why were the most desirable women always the most forbidden? It was against his rules, it was a gigantic bloody risk, but he did what any red-blooded man would have done. He pushed out his chair, stood up and smiled down at her.

'Do you feel like dancing?'

CHAPTER SIX

KISSING Connor O'Brien had been thrilling. Dancing with him was a wild, erotic rush on a dreamy floating ride to...

Desire.

'How deep is your love?' the song called to Sophy's blood, as irresistibly as the moon beckoned the sea. She allowed him to lead her onto the tiny crowded dance floor, and for a breathless moment faced him, the night an elixir in her veins. O'Brien surveyed her with his dark, seductive gaze, then slipped his arm around her waist and pulled her close.

His familiar feel and scent thrilled in her senses in a potent reminder of the kiss. At first, remembering what a fool she'd made of herself then, she tried to hold herself aloof, not to inhale his thrilling, spicy maleness, not to be so conscious of his lithe, athletic body, the long, powerful thighs burning into hers.

'Relax,' he murmured against her ear, his hand firm and sure in the small of her back. 'Just dance.' His mouth brushed her ear, her senses swayed, and she surrendered herself and melted into him. He gave a deep sigh, and drew her closer.

And it was intoxicating. His chest against her breasts. His fingers caressing her spine, stealing into her nape, his hard, angular frame, the occasional brush of his knees, his lips in her hair.

Dancing was such a good excuse for touching. She'd heard of

women who could dance all night held in a man's arms, suspended in a dream. She must have been made of different stuff, because for her it became too difficult. Too—sexual. Or maybe those women hadn't been dancing with Connor O'Brien.

He gazed down at her, his eyes heavy-lidded and aflame, and her lips dried in yearning for his sexy mouth.

His shadow-roughened jaw grazed her temple, and inside her strapless bra her nipples swelled and peaked with shameless longing. All at once she felt the thrust of his arousal against her and her desire ignited as if she were drunk and out of control.

She panicked and pushed him, broke from his arms. 'It's too hot,' she said breathlessly, turning away from the dark flame in his eyes, 'much too hot.'

She stood still amidst the noise and motion of the crowd, her heart thudding, smoothing down her hair and dress with trembly fingers, then with a glance at him threaded her way from the dance floor. He followed without touching her, but in some intangible way she felt the arousing textures of him on her skin as if she were still in his arms.

Back at their table, while she poured the last of the water into her glass, Connor signalled the waiter. With cool efficiency he settled the bill, avoiding looking at Sophy. To her intense disappointment, he stood up and drew out his car keys.

'Ready to leave?' he said, finality in his decisive tone. 'I'll take you home.'

She shrugged and collected her purse, regretting her ridiculous flight from the dance floor. Why had she done it? How uncool he must think her. How naive, when it had felt so fantastic, being held in his arms. It was barely even midnight. If he took her home now, the evening would be over, and there'd never be another one.

She could hardly suggest another dance.

Rising from the table, she turned to look down at the beach. The moon had climbed higher now, and its golden glow had paled to a silver shimmer, finding an occasional glitter in the dark sea. Below the beach wall the sand gleamed softly white.

Connor started to move away, and on a sudden breathless impulse she said, 'It is a shame, though, to go home early on such a beautiful night.'

She saw him pause, tension in the set of his wide shoulders. After a couple of thumping heartbeats he half turned, the keys jingling in his hand, and she felt the flare of heat as he flicked her a glance from beneath his black lashes. His voice was deeper than ever. 'Well…what would you like to do?' His eyes followed her gaze to the beach.

'Perhaps—a walk?'

He hesitated. She could sense conflict in him, the tensing of muscle, the struggle against hard-headed purpose, but with a deep nervous tremor of excitement she knew he would come. After a moment he slipped his car keys back into his pocket, and her spirits rose, along with her anticipation.

Without touching, they descended from the terrace and crossed the grass verge and the beach walk. On the steps down to the beach she paused to slip off her heels, then stepped onto the sand, wriggling her toes, sighing with the bliss of its cool, silken feel under her feet.

'Gorgeous,' she exclaimed. 'Don't you want to take off your shoes?'

His face was shuttered. 'What for?'

'Well,' she said, spreading her arms, and twirling, 'to enjoy it all to the utmost.' She held her face up to the moon and inhaled the salty sea air. 'Smell the smells, hear the roar, feel the spray on your face. Isn't this the ultimate sensual experience?'

His eyes glinted. 'It's *one* ultimate sensual experience. Don't tell me you're one of those people affected by moonlight.'

'Well, I *am* a Piscean.' She smiled at him. Though his eyes burned, they were deeper than ever, mysterious pools. She held out her hand to him, and he shoved his in his pockets. Her heart gave a nervous lurch. She felt suddenly out of her depth. What would she talk about to him, a man she hardly knew, on a beach?

She strolled along with him, away from the hotel and the bright lights. The tide was low, and she followed his lead down to the hard-packed sand on the water line where walking was easier.

Occasional voices floated on the air as people strolled up on the walkway, enjoying the cooler air after their restaurants and entertainments, but the beach itself was deserted, apart from herself and Connor.

The moonlit angles of his face gave him a moody, remote beauty. Even without touching him she could feel the electric tension in his big, lean frame. It connected with hers, in every nerve cell of her body, despite the wall he'd put up. And she could sense his reluctance. Maybe that was why she needed to fill up the space between them with a stream of reminiscence about the Woodruff family holidays, good times she'd had at the beach with Henry and Bea, funny things that had happened to her as a child.

Listening to her chatter he thawed a little, asked the occasional question, even allowed himself a laugh once or twice. Whatever was eating him, the real Connor was there below the surface, the one who'd charmed her just a few hours earlier and rescued her from her social embarrassment. And all the time she was conscious of the silent conversation underlying the one they were having. The magnetic pull that tautened with every wave that broke on the shore and filled her with an exhilarated suspense.

They had almost reached the big rocks at the foot of the headland, when she was startled by the icy shock of foam rushing to kiss her bare feet.

'Oh,' she shrieked. 'Look out. We've come down too far.'

'The tide's on the turn. Come.' He motioned her away, to follow him further up the beach, into the shadow of the rocks at the base of the headland where the sand was cool and deep.

She ran clumsily after him, sinking ankle deep into sand, giggling when she accidentally stumbled against him. He took her arm and steadied her. The brief brush with his body, his firm grip, sent a yearning shiver though her. For a second his intense dark eyes held her breathless, then she moved away from him, into a patch of moonlight.

She could feel his desire as tangibly as the sand under her feet. And his grim resistance.

Night gave the place a primitive, magic quality that infected her with fever. Every sound and texture—the rush and ebb as little runnels of sea water found their way back between the cracks and crevices of the rocks, the shadowy places in between, the warm, caressing dark—in some way they all connected to her and infected her with excitement. Or perhaps it was Connor O'Brien.

A wildness inhabited her. She overflowed with the need to do something reckless and fantastic. Her limbs, her breasts, were languorous with longing. She felt as if the silver moonlight were inside her, as if her skin should shimmer like the scales of a fish.

She held up her face to the moon and stretched out her arms. She could feel Connor's hot eyes on her, sultry embers in their brooding depths.

'Are you ready to go home yet?' His deep voice sounded strained, as if he longed for the answer against his will.

'No.' She laughed giddily, and tilted her head back, stretching out her arms and closing her eyes to bathe in the magic light. 'Don't take me away yet, Connor. I'm drinking in the moonglow.'

'What are you? A witch?' A huskiness had crept into his voice.

With a thundering heart she heard him draw near. She opened her eyes and her pulse skidded as she read the desire in his burning dark gaze.

For a moment he stood as rigid as the rock-face, his handsome face taut and intent, then he reached out and touched her arm with his finger. The vibrant connection sparked an immediate leap in her flesh. As though unable to tear his hand away, he traced her arm and the line of her shoulder to her neck, sparking a trail of fire in her quivering skin.

'You're made of alabaster.' She could hear the dark turbulence in his voice, in his heavy, controlled breathing.

She had no hope of controlling hers. She was trembling, her heart pounding with a tumultuous beat. 'No,' she breathed. 'Just flesh and blood.'

His hands closed around her arms, then he pulled her against him and brought his mouth down on hers in a searing, hungrily possessive kiss. Her blood leaped in immediate response, madly coursing to inflame her nipples and her private, intimate regions.

This was it, she thought. Her time had come.

Wildfire danced along her lips, inside her mouth, wherever his marauding tongue touched the tender, erotic tissues. The taste and scent of him, his big solid body pressed against her, felt so voluptuously sensual she writhed in his arms, grasped at his powerful shoulders, clutched restlessly at his silky, thick hair.

She was ablaze. Her skin felt so sensitised, she thrilled to every touch of his hot, urgent hands caressing her nape, arousing her breasts, roving over her hips. The delight of his big, firm hands on her body was a sensual revelation. She'd never experienced such arousing pleasure.

And her palms ached for the feel of his bare skin. Tentatively, she released a couple of his shirt buttons and slid her hand in to touch his chest. The heat of his skin scorched her palm. Her fingers found the jagged scar over his ribs and she felt a deep tremor rock his big body.

She drew back, searching his dark face, but he was in the grip of a primitive concentration. He pulled her hard against his pelvis and ground his hips against her so she could feel the rigid length of his erection. Desire flared between her thighs. It was so intensely arousing, she couldn't have run now if she'd wanted to. Mesmerised by the dark magic of his mouth on her throat, her breasts, his hands on her wild, feverish body, she clung to him, thirsting for more.

She'd never been touched so intimately. He slipped his hand under her dress and stroked her bottom through her pants. The tingling fire rippled through her flesh and made her crave for his questing fingers to travel further and satisfy her delicious ache.

He kissed her again, open-mouthed, tongues teasing, then when she was nearly ready to faint with the pleasure of him drowning her senses with his heady masculine flavours, he drew back to gaze at her, his dark eyes flaming with a piercing sensuality, as if to appraise how ready she was for further delights. 'You're gorgeous,' he said, breathing hard, his deep voice rough with the passion contained like a powder keg within his powerful body. 'Who could resist you?'

He drew her further into the shadows and she went willingly, thrilling with anticipation as the passion momentum prepared to escalate.

He pulled her down onto the sand with him and slipped her straps from her shoulders, kissing the places where they'd been. Then he trailed tender, sizzling little kisses along the bodice-line of her breast, down to the dip at her cleavage. The sensation of his lips and shadow-roughened jaw on the tender skin of her breasts sent her wild. Half swooning while he stroked her with one hand, she felt him pull at her zip with the other.

Her bodice slipped a little and she felt the air on her naked breasts. He drew back a little, then sighed and gave a deep groan. 'God, Sophy Woodruff. You're too beautiful.'

He stroked her breasts, then took them in his hands and kissed them, tasting the hard nipples, to her amazement nipping them with his *teeth*. Astonishingly, her desire fanned to such a blazing inferno she kneeled up and clutched his shoulders, kissing his mouth and pressing wild, passionate kisses into his strong, bronzed neck and all over his gorgeous powerful chest as if she were a starving virago, ready to eat him alive.

He gave little shudders of pleasure, groaning and half laughing at the same time. Suddenly he put his arms around her and pressed her to him. Then he laid her down on the sand with him and kissed her mouth with such fierce, tender passion she felt as if he were drawing her very soul from her body.

'Connor,' she whispered urgently when the kiss broke and she'd dragged in some air. Her body was on fire with a reckless yearning. 'Do everything to me.'

He gazed at her intently, then sat up. 'Here. Lie on this.' He took off his jacket and spread it on the sand for her.

He stretched beside her, leaning up on his elbow while he unbuckled his belt. In the shadowy light she saw the hot gleam in his dark eyes, but she felt shy about watching him lower his trousers, and looked the other way.

With a potent, sensual touch his hand travelled up from her knee, under her dress, then paused when he connected with the edge of her pants. Thrillingly, he traced the elastic edge around her thigh with one finger, pausing when he reached her inner thigh. She stilled with the tingling anticipation, not daring to move in case he stopped. Then he stroked her with his fingers, through the flimsy material. The pleasure was so intense, she gasped and panted in quick, shallow breaths. Just when her excitement mounted to an almost unbearable pitch, he bent to kiss her from her navel down to her pants, igniting fire wherever his lips touched. He paused at her pants' upper edge. The delicious suspense became excruciating, then he suddenly tweaked them down, right down over her knees to her ankles.

She lay on the sand, naked from the waist down, her heart thundering in her chest. She'd never felt so exposed, and was glad Connor O'Brien couldn't see her blushing like a teenager. Even in the dark, though, she could see the flame lighting his eyes, and appreciated with tremulous gratitude that this was her moment to be a real woman, to make an adult exchange with a man without fear or shame.

And such a man. The moonlight cast certain planes and angles of his face into relief, highlighting the severe lines of his hard, masculine beauty.

His slumbrous gaze rested on her nest of dark curls, and he began to stroke her there. After what she'd participated in already, she knew her reluctance to part her thighs was unreasonable, but she kept them pressed firmly together. Connor didn't seem to mind, though. His eyes just gleamed the brighter.

Casting her a seductive, smiling glance, he bent to, oh, so softly kiss the dark tangled curls. Then gently, teasingly, he slipped his hand between her thighs, and she let him part them.

He paused to search his trouser pockets, then after a muttered exclamation glanced up at her. 'Do you have anything with you?'

His deep voice was darker than the shadows in the cliff-face. She heard a wave crash with what sounded like increased ferocity, the surge and retreat of swirling foam as it was sucked irresistibly back into the boiling surf.

'What do you mean?'

'Protection.' He spoke softly, but there was an urgency in his tone as he added, 'Condoms.'

She widened her eyes. 'Me? No.'

Breathless moments ticked by while he scanned her face with his hot, hungry gaze, then he drew away from her and sat up. 'Ah…hell.'

She leaned up on her elbows and touched his arm. 'Don't you have any?'

'I thought I did, but, no.'

His disappointment was so apparent, she exclaimed, 'I'm sorry, Connor. I didn't expect… I've never thought to… I've never had any reason to carry them.'

He gave his head a wry shake. 'And you a feminist.' Then he cast an appraising glance over her and smiled, lilting his brows. 'There are, of course, other ways.'

'How do you mean?'

She flushed then, realising how naive the question had been. For goodness' sake, how many issues of *Cosmo* had spelled it all out? How many fascinating post-mortems had she sat through with the girls over the breakfast table?

She corrected herself swiftly, 'I mean, of *course*. I know there are.'

His eyes glinted and narrowed on her face. She felt the sudden blood beat in her ears as a small frown gathered between his brows.

'What did you mean when you said you've never had any reason?'

She supposed she'd have to admit this sooner or later. She sat up and pulled down her dress, held her bodice up with one arm to cover her breasts. 'Just that I…' Her cheeks felt hot. Lucky it was quite dark. 'Well, you know, I haven't actually slept with anyone before.'

He stared at her, blinking. 'What?' He stilled to rigidity. For a second his lean frame could have been carved in stone. Then he let out a groan. 'My God. Tell me you're not saying you're a virgin.'

She'd always known there'd be a moment to admit this, and it might be embarrassing. Shaming, even. She was probably the oldest virgin in Sydney, possibly Australia. But, ever the eternal optimist, she'd always hoped *he*, whoever he was, would just accept it.

Gazing at him now, he looked anything *but* accepting. Her heart was pounding, but this time with an accelerating anxiety. Loath to show it, though, she said, 'It doesn't make any difference, does it? I mean, as you say, I can still… We—*we* can still make love, however you say… I'll—I'll do—whatever… Whatever you…'

Connor heard the tremor as her voice trailed off. The rock-hard, throbbing reality of his desire hardened further to taunt him. He saw her mouth swollen with his kisses, saw the sudden lowering of her lashes over her glittering gaze, and burned to have her.

But, God almighty, whatever his sins, he had some sort of a conscience. He forced himself to turn sharply from her and dragged himself to his feet, disappointment eating into his soul like bile.

'Connor…' He heard shame in her voice and his gut squirmed as his pain reached a crescendo.

'Don't talk to me. Don't look at me,' he ground out. 'Go away from me. Take yourself away.'

In the raw silence that followed as she stood up behind him and fixed her dress, his thought processes clicked in and helped a little in the cruel dousing of his erection.

How could he have allowed himself to succumb? Once he'd had her, he'd never keep her at arm's length. She'd want more. For God's sake, *he'd* want more. Impossible visions flashed through his mind—seeing her every day at the Alexandra, picking her up at her place, taking her to his place…

Familiarity, intimacy. Involvement.

And the things she'd said. *Make love*, as if they were a couple. Hell, she'd expect him to be her boyfriend.

An unbidden image of her nude body lying in that big empty bed flashed through his brain, and he struggled to banish it. As he buttoned his shirt, fastened his clothes over his aching arousal, he forced himself to concentrate on non-sexual things. On seaweed, and rocks and the creeping tide. On his rules and his unwavering commitment. On responsibility, and broken bodies and his hollow, broken life.

He picked up his jacket and shook it. Her innocence had been plain to see from the start. When had he ever got it so wrong? It was all his own fault. He'd seduced her to this point and now she had hopes of him. *We can still make love* echoed in his brain like a reproach.

He should never have given into temptation. He deserved to be shot.

When it felt safe enough, halfway at least, he looked around to see where she'd got to. She was a long way down, walking up the beach towards the steps, shoes dangling from her fingers. Her proud head, her slender neck looked so achingly vulnerable in the moonlight he felt something twist in his chest.

He caught up to her before she reached the hotel steps. 'I'll drive you home.'

'I'll get a cab.'

'No, *I'll* take you home,' he said, cool and ruthless as he had to be, knowing he was a brute. He would rue it all in the tortured night to come, cringe when he recalled his necessary savagery. 'You'll never get a cab out here at this hour.'

Ignoring her refusal, he guided her with brusque purpose through the hotel to the car park. He asked her for directions, although of course he knew the way.

The trip to Neutral Bay was silent with strain, but he made no effort to alleviate it. The more she suffered, the better for her in the long run.

He drew up in the silent leafy street in front of the old federation-style house, as if for the first time. He felt her glance as he pulled on the handbrake, and saw her hand reach for the door handle, ready for a quick escape.

'Thanks…'

'Don't thank me,' he said harshly, shamed by her good manners. He got out and went around to open her door, watched her slide out, walk past him to the gate without looking at him.

'Don't bother to come in,' she threw over her shoulder.

Stung, though he knew he deserved the worst, he still felt the need to insist, 'I'll walk you to the door.'

He followed her up a honeysuckle-scented path at the side of the house to where a light glowed on a porch. She bent to retrieve her key from a flowerpot. Even this evidence of her sweet humanity added to the black weight building in his chest. As she struggled with the lock he saw that her slim hands were shaking, and his darkness intensified.

'I won't come in,' he said when she'd got the door open, in case she still harboured expectations.

She gave him a withering look and started to close the door.

'Wait.' He shoved his foot in the crack and reefed his fingers through his hair while he tried to think of an exit. 'Sophy—let me explain.'

Her eyes glittered in the shadowy light. 'Don't,' she replied in her low, husky voice. 'You don't need to explain. I should thank *you* for dinner.'

'Oh, Sophy.' Guilt riddled him with holes. 'Look… You are a—a very beautiful woman. I shouldn't have allowed your charms to overwhelm my good sense tonight. I think we were both affected by that damned moon.'

She made to close the door, but he caught her and pulled her towards him.

'Sweetheart.' He held her arms, feeling the trembling of her smooth body in his hands. He had the shamed sensation he was crushing something fragile. Why did she have to be so damned desirable? He watched the play of shadows on her face and felt himself being drawn back on the same wild riptide, almost unbearably tempted to kiss her and start it all over again. 'I don't want any kind of… I don't *do* involvements. I'm not the guy for you. It's—nothing personal.'

She twisted from his grasp. 'And there was I, thinking you were the man of my dreams. What a let-down.'

The gentle sarcasm triggered a slight rise in his blood pressure. He was glad it was too dark for her to see his sudden flush. He resisted the temptation to shift his glance, and stated with grim finality, 'I'm not a man for anyone's dreams.'

She stayed silent. That discomfiting light was in her eyes, as if she could see straight through him.

'Look,' he asserted, 'we'll forget all about tonight. Put it out of our minds. Nothing happened. There's no harm done. All right?'

Gently, but very firmly, she closed the door in his face.

CHAPTER SEVEN

SOPHY saw him the morning after, far too soon for her lacerated feelings. She was at the top of the stairs directing one of her parents to the basement coffee shop, when her stomach clenched. Connor O'Brien appeared, elegant in a charcoal suit, briefcase in hand, strolling along the gallery towards his office. In the same charged instant he saw her. His long, easy stride almost checked, then continued on, as fluid as ever.

He flashed her a smooth, untroubled greeting as he unlocked his office door. Somehow she forced herself to respond with her own punishing brand of cool.

It took ages for her galloping pulse to slow down. She retreated to her office and tried uselessly to concentrate on a report she needed to write about the young child she'd just seen. It was a strain, with her insides so sore and aching.

Unfortunately, she couldn't think of anything else except Connor. Typical, she supposed, for someone as green and gauche and naive as she'd been on that beach. Much as she wished she could wipe the excruciating events from her mind, she couldn't eradicate him from her senses. Everything he'd said, every kiss and caress, seemed branded into her.

She wasn't sure why she should feel such a sense of failure. Certainly, she was the only woman in Australia who could go to a moonlit beach at midnight with a sexy man and come home *virgo intacta*. It was a pity about the condoms, but it hadn't needed to have ended there. She'd have done anything he wanted if he'd only explained a little.

But, oh, *God*... She covered her face with her hands. If only she hadn't *told* him that.

She cringed to think of how put off he'd been. It was clear she'd disgusted him with her over-enthusiasm. And why had she behaved that way, like a wild, obsessed creature? Her insides squirmed in mortification as she remembered some of her wanton behaviour, and she had to get up and pace the room with her hands on her burning cheeks to walk the agony out of her system.

He had fancied her at the start, she was certain. There was no mistaking that. Even now, remembering the scorching desire in his eyes made her insides curl over. According to all the women's magazines she'd ever read, men *liked* passionate women. Even if they were virgins.

So why not her?

And why had he said those things to her at the end? All that stuff about involvement. It wasn't as if she'd asked him to marry her, was it?

A thought she'd been fending off since her agonised walk back across the moonlit sand clawed at the vital depths of her feminine being. She'd always understood that males were so driven by their passions, a man would be unlikely to refuse sex when it was on offer. Yet last night...

Could it be that at the critical moment, when it had come to the crunch, Connor O'Brien hadn't found her sexy?

Dismay sank through her like icewater. If only there were someone she could talk to about it. But, no, even if Zoe and Leah weren't away on holiday now, she could never admit her debacle. She could never talk about it to anyone, not even Zoe.

Elliott Fraser phoned during the morning, with apologies that for him were quite profuse. He explained his housekeeper had been called away on a family emergency and there'd been no one at home to look after his son. She felt mollified, in a listless sort of way. There could hardly be a better excuse than that. At least he'd put Matthew's safety first.

What he said next, though, might have given her wilting optimism a boost, if she hadn't been so good at listening between the lines. Elliott still felt the need to discuss their 'situation', and he wondered if she would be prepared to visit him at his home.

He went on to explain that since the housekeeper's availability was uncertain, and since it was urgent to lock down the 'problem'—*her*, Sophy supposed—and since they couldn't be seen meeting at their places of work and needed a private venue for a longer discussion, his house was the most reasonable available meeting place.

His house.

Great. Maybe.

For once, possibly because of the ache weighing on her heart, she had trouble keeping up her spirits during the conversation. The language Elliott had used clearly signalled his intention to tidy her away like an embarrassing nuisance. At one stage, as he'd talked, her pride had nearly propelled her into snapping, 'Oh, look. Forget I ever bothered you,' and hanging up on him.

She was glad she'd controlled the impulse, though. If she'd given into that one, she'd have lost all the headway, if any, she'd made so far, and any chance of getting to know her little brother.

So she agreed. Dinner, he'd said. He'd phone her again with a suitable night. She wondered who would cook it if the housekeeper wasn't there. Somehow, she couldn't imagine Elliott doing something so comfortable and hospitable himself.

After lunch, once the sun had gone off the window ledge she took a few minutes to water her drooping geraniums. It was then that she was shaken by another realisation.

The letter.

With all her anguish over Connor O'Brien, she'd forgotten about it. She tried to imagine confessing to Elliott, but after his hostile tone last night the thought made her go cold. The beastly thing was almost certainly still hiding in Connor's office where she must have lost it the day Millie moved. How long before he found it? And he *knew* Elliott's father. If he read it… She nearly went faint as the connections slotted together with lightning speed. Connor would inform the older man. Of course he would. He'd tell him his son had a daughter.

How repulsed, how unforgiving Elliott would be if his father told him he knew all about his love child, and he'd heard it from an old friend of the family.

She started to sweat, and it was nothing to do with the heatwave. For an insane moment she even considered asking Connor to search for the letter for her. Thank goodness her pride clicked in before she succumbed to that fatal impulse. With a sharp ache she realised she could never talk to him again.

There was nothing else for it. Somehow, whatever else happened, she'd have to find a way to retrieve it herself.

'So what's she like?'

Perhaps because of all the trees and shady pathways, Taronga Zoo seemed like an oasis in the heat. The air had turned more humid, and a few lowering clouds were bunched on the horizon, as if the long-awaited change might be in the offing.

Connor paused with Sir Frank to watch a giraffe's graceful floating glide across its enclosure on long, spindly legs. Legs that yearned for wide-open spaces. He frowned, troubled as always by helpless creatures. Beyond the animals' prison a snapshot view of Sydney Harbour shimmered in the searing sun, the iron span of the bridge hanging between two shores like a gigantic cat's cradle. Could a view compensate for freedom?

Sir Frank walked with the aid of a stick, his shrunken frame barely reaching Connor's shoulder. An excited seven-year-old tearing down the path ahead of his family group nearly barrelled into them. Connor grabbed the old guy and moved him out of harm's way.

'Don't they love it, even in this heat?' the old man marvelled when Connor had steadied him and the kid had been retrieved by a young woman with another child in a stroller. 'I could have brought Matthew if it hadn't been a pre-school day. This is one of our favourite haunts.' He popped a mint into his mouth and turned his beady gaze back to Connor. 'What did you say she was like?'

A virgin, was Connor's first knee-jerk response. Unavoidable, really, since lately he'd been giving virgins a great deal of thought. Not that he was a man who'd ever cared about such things. He wasn't sure he'd ever actually *had* a virgin.

He gave Sir Frank a straight look. 'Slim. Five-seven. Dark hair.'

He tried to fight it, but his thoughts insisted on returning to their honeyed trap. Translucent skin, softer than a peach's. Ripe breasts, exactly the fit for a man's hand. His fingers curled involuntarily into his palm. Sweet raspberry nipples…

'Beautiful? She'd have to be to compare with Marla.'

Connor forced himself not to react. 'Attractive enough, I suppose.' But a pang at his grudging admission sliced through him as the image that tortured his nights flashed into his head. Sophy Woodruff's face, her eyes shadowed with desire, lashes heavy and languorous, her smiling, edible mouth, meltingly eager for love.

Sir Frank shot him a glance. 'Well? What have you found?'

'She was born in Brisbane, family moved to Sydney at nine.' Conscious of the old guy's almost supernatural perspicacity, he carefully cut all expression from his tone. 'Grew up in Neutral Bay, still lives in the same house. Educated at local schools, attended Sydney University. Her parents are modest people, Beatrice and Henry Woodruff, currently out of the country. No siblings. She shares the house with two friends. Both nurses. I've checked and they're clean of all known connections. All of them.'

'*All?*' The old man's brows rose, then he nodded, accepting Connor's word. 'Right, right. I see. So?'

So what? Was she Elliott Fraser's lover? Not unless she was an Oscar-worthy actress. He hunched and shoved his hands in his pockets, tried not to think of the beach.

'It's not an affair,' he said curtly, anxious to move on from what was not his finest hour.

'What?' The old guy stopped, clearly surprised. 'Are you sure?'

Connor looked squarely at him. 'As sure as anyone can be.'

Perhaps he sounded a little terse, but the heat alone would make anyone short of temper. An urgency to call the whole thing off seized him. He felt a sudden anger that his precious isolation was being threatened by what was, after all, just an old man's suspicions. Wasn't he supposed to dedicate his skills to the security of his country? Who cared if Elliott Fraser made a fool of himself? Would the country be worse off?

Sir Frank frowned and shook his head. 'Then *what* is it? If it's not an affair— Are you definite she's not an operative? Have you searched her home?'

Connor bunched his fists in his pockets. He'd put off that distasteful task. For God's sake, what was he, a spook in some television show?

'She's a speech therapist in a children's clinic. She's bound by some kind of commitment not to speak about her connection with Elliott. Whatever it is—he's the one calling the shots. My guess is—it's something to do with the boy.' He paused in the shade of a mulberry tree overhanging the wombat enclosure and drew out the keys to his rooms. 'Here, Sir Frank.' He held them out. 'This is hardly my field. Hire a private investigator. Some bloke who doesn't mind peeping into windows and taking photographs.'

The old man eyed him for a moment, then waved the keys away. 'No fear, matey. What are you saying? You can deal with terrorists and assassins, but you haven't the stomach to check up on a girl?'

'A woman,' Connor corrected sharply. 'She's a woman.' He

glanced at Sir Frank and saw the old guy looking at him with that curiously penetrating stare he was famous for.

'*Is* she? Well, then. Do what nature cut you out for. Sweet-talk her. Use a device on her phones. Bug the woman's bedroom. You're so edgy, fella, a bit of feminine company might be just exactly what you need.'

Connor's intestines clenched, everything in him repulsed by the thought of spying on her as if she were some dangerous criminal. As if she were the one at fault. As if…

As if, for God's sake, after his treatment of her she would ever look at him again with anything except contempt.

Though he knew very well that, on the other hand—certainly in his case—fruit once tasted, then forbidden, only grew sweeter in the memory. His eyes drifted shut.

Sweeter, more irresistible, more mouth-wateringly desirable. And how much more would that obsessive hunger tug at her, a woman who'd tasted passion for the first time?

A virgin.

He crushed down a pang of shame at his brutal behaviour on the beach night. A woman's first experience with love was supposed to be so powerful as to be unforgettable. Hell, he could even remember *his* first time. What would Sophy Woodruff be likely to associate with her first real taste of sex? Until…

Oh, God. He let out a sudden breath.

Until some new guy came along and wiped the mess from her mind. There'd be someone along, soon enough. Some guy who was freely available to get involved. Hopefully, one with some finesse as a lover. Unaccountably, his gut tightened at the thought.

Virgins required tenderness. Sophy Woodruff needed a lover who could take her in hand and teach her gently how to enjoy her body. How to wring every ounce of pleasure from that luscious arrangement of curves. Someone who could take the time to arouse her properly, and take her to the heights…

He hoped the old guy's eerie prediction wasn't coming true. In an unnerving flash he visualised his precious objectivity as a fine porcelain plate, revealing the first fine, microscopic line that presaged a crack.

He clenched his hands. The only honourable way forward he could see now, the only safe way, was to leave town. Remove himself entirely from the scene, let her get on with her life, while he got on with his.

Such as it was.

He opened his mouth to inform Sir Frank he was bailing out, but the octogenarian must have been reading his mind, for he pursed his lips, nodding his head and musing, 'I suppose if the worst happened and you pulled out, I *could* pay some private detective.'

'*No.*' Connor's immediate reaction burst from a visceral level before he could control it. But the idea of some other guy striking up an acquaintance with her, tailing her, invading her bedroom, rifling through her things with his grubby fingers—her sweet, feminine, virginal things—was intolerable.

Surely—better himself than some sleazy amateur.

Noting Sir Frank's look of surprise, he made a swift effort to recover his cool, and injected some sense into the discussion. 'You don't want a stranger checking up on Elliott, do you? Who knows what he might find out?'

'That's true, that's true,' the old man replied, nodding sagely. 'You're right, Connor, it had better be you. And, look, son, choose any method you like. I know you'll get results.' His brow creased into a thousand worry lines. 'You know, however innocent it might look on the surface, I've got a very strong hunch there's something significant going on here.'

Sir Frank's driver hoved into view, walking towards them to collect the ancient and carry him off for his lunch. Connor waited a moment to watch Parkins aid the old guy's slow progress up the path in case he needed a hand, then, satisfied, turned down the slope towards the ferry wharf, lost in reflection.

Instead of relinquishing the task as he'd intended, somehow he found himself sunk in even deeper, like a man caught in quicksand. He would just have to ensure he was never alone with her again. The temptation was too great.

She might avert her face now when he passed her by in the gallery, but he could recall only too vividly the fire that lay buried beneath that ice.

He gave a rueful shrug. Virgins might believe they could douse the flames of desire by freezing a man out. It only went to show how much they had to learn about the male animal.

The breath suspended in his lungs at an unbidden thought. How—how very easily he could reignite that blaze.

Not that he would. It was simply a case of self-discipline.

CHAPTER EIGHT

ANOTHER Friday dawned, heavy and humid. Fog had rolled in through the night and wrapped the world in a shroud. On the ferry across to Circular Quay Sophy felt as if the damp had seeped into her soul. When the cloud finally dissipated, it left behind a sultry, brooding heat, as if some sullen fury were building and plotting to vent its vengeance on the world.

Even the Alexandra was overly warm. In fact, her very computer felt hot when she switched it on, as if it had already done half a day's work before she arrived. For a second she wondered if Cindy or one of the doctors had been in there, searching her files for something, then dismissed the notion. They'd never do that.

At morning tea she considered not going down to the basement to buy coffee, but couldn't sacrifice the opportunity to walk past Connor O'Brien's office and find out if he was there.

Maybe—she allowed herself the shameful admission—she'd run into him. She wished she could cut him out of her mind and go back to being her ordinary careless self, but now her awareness of him seemed to infuse everything she did, had turned her into a vessel of yearning. She kept imagining she could see his lean, handsome figure in crowds. Once, returning early from netball, she'd even thought she spotted him driving down her street. Another night, lying curled up on her bed in sleepless longing, she felt such a powerful and haunting sense of his presence that when she finally did drop off to sleep, she dreamed of him there in her room, picking up her pillow and burying his face in it.

Crazy. She was turning into a madwoman. It was just as the girls had predicted. She'd gone completely overboard, and was utterly unable to swim.

Whenever she encountered Connor's tall figure approaching in the Alexandra, one look at his moody, darkly handsome face and her insides suffered a seismic shock. By the time she'd pulled herself together to say something coherent, he had passed by, and the moment was lost.

It was clear she needed to be more prepared. But how was she to behave? She felt as if he were holding her at a distance with his will, and there was nothing she could do about it. The rejectee could hardly take the initiative.

What she needed was a plan. A way to show him she was not succumbing to humiliation over the beach thing. Not a campaign, exactly, so much as a statement of confidence in her sex appeal.

She started with clothes. She'd read dozens of magazine articles that showed how a woman could project her sensuality in the workplace while still appearing demure and professional. Fitted shapes, rich colours and sensuous fabrics could swathe the feminine body in elegance while subtly calling to the male. Higher heels, lipstick, perfume and, above all, a cool, tranquil attitude. It was too hot to plant anything in the garden, anyway, so she'd actually spent the previous weekend combing the shops.

She introduced the new items sparingly into her daily wardrobe, so as not to alert anyone's suspicion. Most of her efforts were wasted, though. However cool and sensual she appeared in her sashays along the gallery, Connor was too often away from his office to notice. He seemed to be out most days, and only appeared late in the afternoon when everyone was leaving.

The truth was, he was avoiding her.

She knew she shouldn't let it, but it hurt like hell. Only yesterday she'd been lunching under the willow in the Gardens with a few of the girls from the next floor down, and looked up to see him strolling through, heading somewhere. He'd seen her and swerved away to take another path. She'd felt such a savage stab in her chest then she'd scarcely been able to breathe.

But she knew she had to conquer the feelings and stay in control of her life. She had clients depending on her, her normal contacts to keep up, and now that she'd started the Elliott Fraser process there could be no turning back from that. However difficult, she had to grit her teeth and see it through.

Her decision to go for coffee that morning paid off, in one way, although it cut her to shreds in another. When she walked out into the gallery, Connor was outside his office in conversation with Cindy. He had his briefcase in his hand, looking devastating and sophisticated in a charcoal suit. Despite everything, it would still have been such a charge to see him, if he hadn't been smiling and listening intently to something their receptionist was telling him. She supposed she could hardly blame him. Cindy *was* very pretty and bubbly. And now she was calling him 'O'Brien', as if they were mates.

Friends.

As Sophy approached the two of them Cindy broke off talking. It almost seemed as if they'd been talking about *her*. When Connor glanced up at her, his smile faded and his dark eyes grew intense and impenetrable. There was something so hungry and primitive in that look her body plunged into a wild surge of bittersweet excitement.

But for once she managed to ignore her blood's sudden frenzied pounding to smile coolly and glide by like the Queen of the Nile. She felt glad to be wearing high heels and a cherry-red silk dress like a cheong-sam. It fastened demurely to its mandarin collar, and had a longish hidden split in the side that allowed occasional flashes of leg. She didn't have to look around to know his eyes were following her.

* * *

Afterwards, to banish the image of Sophy Woodruff in a red dress, Connor took refuge in his office and updated his case notes on the progress of the 'Djara Djara People versus New South Wales'. The claims and counterclaims of the case had drawn on for years. He could see at a glance that the Djara Djara needed stronger representation if they were to win in the High Court. They'd never be able to afford someone like him, so the work would have to be donated. But how fantastic it would be to help them to reclaim their traditional lands. At one time he'd actually been keen to dedicate his own skills to their cause.

Before he was headhunted by Foreign Affairs. And then a plane had crashed over Syria, his world had turned into a charred ruin, and everything had changed.

On a sudden, rare impulse he felt for his wallet, opened it and drew out the photo taken in Paris six years ago. Somehow the portrait had captured the sunshine lighting their blonde heads and wrapped them in a joyous halo, though the effect wasn't as noticeable now as it once had been. He grimaced to himself. For a long time he hadn't been able to bear to examine it at all, now it seemed he'd grown out of the habit of trying.

He frowned at the faces, familiar now he had them before him. Strange though, how even the most beloved faces could fade in the recollection.

He laid the photo on the desk and returned to the Djara Djara. Their case was compelling. If he hadn't chosen to complicate his work for the embassy with the challenges of covert operations...

Still, it was done now. He'd accepted the agency's recruitment invitation, plunged into the gruelling training regimen—telescoped into a third of the time normally required of agents—and made the commitment to file intelligence reports. He hadn't diverged from his career path, merely taken on another that had led him into some strange and torturous situations.

After the crash there'd been a weird sort of symmetry in signing up for more danger in one of the most hazardous hotspots on the planet. He'd avoided admitting it to Sir Frank, but now, from this distance, the tightrope he trod over there was starting to look like sheer lunacy.

Still, nothing felt as crazy as the nights he'd spent sitting parked in a street in Neutral Bay, while Sophy Woodruff slept, imagining her luscious curves and the rise and fall of her breath.

Admit it. *Burning* to be with her in that bed.

If he were free to do as he wanted…

Dammit, if she weren't a virgin. It always came back to that. If she were an experienced woman who understood that a kiss and a night or two between consenting adults didn't have to mean for ever, he might consider reopening negotiations.

But there was no way around it. With her willow trees, her beach walks, her moonglow, she was clearly crazy for romance. Exactly the type to get sucked in deep, while he was honour-bound to maintain his singularity.

Thank God she was keeping her distance. He didn't need any more people on his conscience. He just wished he hadn't seen her in that red dress.

On her side of the wall, Sophy ploughed on through her work. She'd decided to skip lunch in the Gardens. The trouble was, she couldn't get the morning's encounter out of her mind and needed to brood over it. Besides, it was too hot to eat. If it hadn't been for the delightful moments with the children, she doubted if she could have lasted the day.

In the afternoon, clouds started to build on the horizon, and there was the occasional rumble, like a somnolent giant almost ready to surface from a deep, deep sleep. For the first time in days a breeze fanned her cheek.

All through the afternoon the image of Connor O'Brien's disturbing gaze tortured her mind. The distraction slowed her down, so that by the time the others were packing up and leaving for the weekend, she still had reports to finish.

How long could the madness go on? It was affecting her entire life. She'd hardly slept for a week. Twice at netball people had thrown her the ball and it had sailed right past without her even noticing.

If he would only speak to her, about any small thing. Anything to defuse the intolerable suspense. There had to be some way they could talk to each other.

There was, of course, the letter. If she couldn't talk to him, how else was she to retrieve it, still ticking away somewhere in his rooms like a time bomb? Elliott could phone at any moment. What if he chose *this* weekend to invite her to the Fraser home?

At first inconceivable, the last-ditch, desperate possibility of making a bold frontal approach that had been simmering in her mind for days began to take on a seductive appeal. What if she went to Connor's rooms, knocked on his door, and simply asked if she could search? How could he refuse?

They were adults, weren't they? Surely she could request something of him without him assuming she was attempting to lure him. If she made it *absolutely clear* she was no longer attracted… If she could somehow correct the humiliating impression she'd left him with, show clearly that she wasn't a love-sick, sex-starved nympho, yearning for any contact with him, however minuscule.

She returned to her report and tried to concentrate, knowing she couldn't take the risk. His contempt at what would seem like an obvious ploy could destroy her.

Although, if she didn't do *something*, another weekend would go by without any improvement in the situation.

At some level, though, the impulse must have been solidifying in her subconscious, because all at once she whipped around to her bag and raked through it for her comb and lipstick, then rose to check her appearance in the children's wall mirror. She retouched her lips to a rich, ruby red, and retied the ribbon in her nape.

Bracing herself with a deep breath, like an automaton she walked through Reception and out into the empty gallery. Just short of Connor's door her feet slowed like a coward's, but somehow she forced them on.

Standing outside his office, her heart racketing a drum roll, the excoriating thing he'd said at the beach came back and threatened to slay her all over again.

Go away from me. Take yourself away.

For a second her nerve nearly failed. But what was she, a timid child?

She winched up all the courage she possessed, rapped firmly and waited, barely able to breathe, every muscle clenched. She was just considering making a frantic dash back to her office and pretending she'd never left it, when a shape loomed behind the opaque glass, stilled a moment, then the door opened.

Connor O'Brien's dark eyes clashed with hers, then slid over her with a heart-stopping, sensual intensity. But even as his raw, animal magnetism reached out to pull her in and trap every strand of her being in a giddy, yearning coil, his black brows drew together. His expression smoothed into inscrutability and he drew back a little. 'Sophy. Hello.'

She angled her gaze away and managed to articulate, though her throat felt dry and her lips were stiff, 'I hate to take up your time, but I need to get that letter back. I was hoping I could come in for a quick second and look for it.'

He continued to block the doorway for a moment, long enough for her heart to plunge as she registered his reluctance, then he opened it wide. 'Sure.'

He shoved his hands into his pockets, as if to avoid touching her, and she walked past him, careful not to brush against him, and headed through the reception office into his inner sanctum. Her heart was pounding so hard she could hear the beat in her ears. She drew a deep breath, and attempted to fill up the fraught space with words. 'I know I lost it in here. I think it could be—behind something.'

She sensed the high-voltage electric force of his attention, but she kept her face averted so as not to risk being annihilated by meeting sardonic amusement in his eyes. All the time her breathless words continued hurtling forth. 'I helped Millie pack up in here the day before you—moved in. I suppose it must have fallen from my bag. I have a very strong feeling it might have been caught up behind a piece of your furniture.'

She ran out of breath, and there was a jumpy little silence.

She cast a glance about. The room looked more lived in since her last visit. He'd hung some certificates on the walls asserting his credit as a lawyer and a member of the Bar Association. A couple of them displayed his right to practise in the Supreme Court, and the High Court of Australia. The string of letters after his name looked impressive.

He must have been working when she'd interrupted, because the breeze through the open window was gently riffling a pile of papers on his desk. Beside it was an empty coffee cup and an open notebook with notes written in a bold, flowing hand. She couldn't help ogling his things with an insane hunger, and wished she could have touched them.

'Ah. So you have a very strong feeling.' He strolled over to lean his wide shoulders against the wall. 'Well, in that case, it must certainly be in here. Where would you like to start?'

His velvet words couldn't mask the steel implacability of his resistance to her. She felt so conscious of invading his territory, of him being in absolute control. He folded his arms across his chest and she tried not to remember that powerful chest, lit by moonlight, the whorls of masculine hair brushing her breasts.

'Oh, well, the—the filing cabinet, I guess.'

She risked a fleeting glance at him, and the dark eyes dwelling on her face were grave, not at all mocking.

He moved out of the way with extreme politeness, and she approached the cabinet, kneeling down to look behind it without seeing anything there except darkness. She got up then, dusting down her dress, and stood in front of it, grasping the solid piece in an ineffectual attempt to pull it out from the wall. 'What on earth have you got in here?'

Realising her hands were shaking, she quickly lowered them from the cabinet.

'Files. Here,' he said smoothly, and she realised he'd noticed. 'You'd better let me. You wouldn't want to spoil that dress.'

Had there been a sensual note in his deep voice? She dismissed the notion at once as wishful thinking.

She stood aside while he dragged the cabinet out with apparent ease, but when she looked there was nothing behind it except a rind of dust.

He shrugged and pushed it back in place. 'No good. What next?'

It occurred to her then that he didn't believe her instincts about the letter, and was just humouring her. She was seized with the challenge to find it, and prove herself right. Anything to acquit herself of his almost certain assumption that she'd visited him purely because she couldn't stay away.

Energised to succeed, she moved away to check behind everything large and small around the perimeter of the entire room, conscious of his eyes following her.

After a second he said, his deep voice a little hesitant, 'So—how are you? How've you been?'

'Fine, thanks.'

'You *look* very well.'

She didn't answer.

'That…er…that dress suits you.'

She lowered her lashes to hide her heart's leap. 'Thanks.'

'I thought earlier…wondered if you had shadows under your eyes. Has the heat been affecting you?'

She gave him a sardonic glance. Maybe he thought *he* was affecting her. Well, maybe he was, but how dared he assume it?

'I mean, you always look cool, but I just wondered…'

She gave a cool shrug. 'I've been having some late nights.'

His brows lifted. 'Have you? You mean—workwise, or…social?'
She met his gaze full on. 'Purely social.'

His dark eyes scrutinised her face, glinting. For a moment she almost had the feeling he knew exactly how much of a barefaced lie that had been.

She'd reached the massive bookcase. There was a gap of a few centimetres between it and the wall. Pressing her cheek against the wall, she could just make out something on the floor behind the case. It looked promising.

'There is something here.' In her excitement her voice rose a little and she lost some of her constraint. 'Hey, look, this could be it.'

She tried shifting the heavy piece herself, but had no hope of budging it an inch. Connor quickly stepped in to push her out of the way, shoving his shoulder against the case and bracing his powerful legs to ease it from the wall, the tendons straining in his neck with effort until the aperture was wide enough.

As the space opened to the light she saw an envelope with one badly scuffed corner, and with a little cry of triumph pounced on it.

'It *is* it.'

She straightened up, examining it almost with disbelief, turning it over and over. There was her name in the window, Violet Woodruff. She slid the folded letter from inside, and it was exactly as she'd last seen it. 'Well, there you are, now. I told you, didn't I? I was right. What a relief. This is it. This truly is it.'

Connor O'Brien pushed the bookcase back into position and turned to watch her, an enigmatic expression on his lean, handsome face.

'Oh, and look, I'm sorry I accused you of—taking it.' She flushed a little with guilt. 'Of course, I realise you would never do anything like that.'

He lowered his dark lashes to screen his gaze.

The fitful breeze snatched up the papers on his desk and she sprang to secure them, tidying them back into a pile and placing the cup on top to hold them. Her glance fell on a small photograph, partly hidden by the notebook.

Connor must have spotted it at the same time, because he swiftly moved to pick it up and tuck it into his shirt pocket. Their eyes met, and he hesitated for a second, as though about to say something about it, then turned away and went into the front office, murmuring about speaking to the cleaner.

Somehow, though, the breath was knocked from her lungs. She'd only caught one glimpse of the photo, but she'd seen enough to know what it meant.

He was married. Married with a child.

Why hadn't she guessed? It was clearly impossible for a man like him not to have been snapped up long ago. With a dreary inevitability, in her mind she scrolled through every encounter she'd had with him, from that first time in the mothers' room. He didn't wear a ring, and hadn't he told Cindy he was single? So perhaps the photo meant he was divorced. Although, did men keep pictures of their ex-wives handy? Unless...

Unless he was a cheat. A cheat, a liar and a scoundrel who made love to other women besides his wife. Maybe that explained the sense she'd often had that he was concealing something.

She walked across to close the windows, placing her letter on the sill while she knelt on the desk to reach out for the window catch. Just as she leaned out a gust of wind snatched the letter up and wafted it off the sill.

Thank goodness it only landed on the ledge outside. Grateful for her split, she half straddled the sill, and stooped to pick the thing up. But the instant before her fingers connected with it, another gust lifted it and skidded it along the ledge a little way past the window casement.

In a split-second reflex she climbed gingerly out all the way, and edged along the ledge until she'd nearly reached it, clinging to the window casement, then beyond that the wall. Each time she was nearly upon the letter, it moved on a little further. That beastly letter had become an allegory for her life, she reflected. Just when she thought she had it all, it slipped from her fingers and she had to go after it again.

The surface of the sandstone was amazingly rough. She dug her fingers in, conscious of the stone scouring her fingertips, grazing her cheek, adhering to the silk fabric of her dress.

At last the letter remained stationary long enough for her to reach it. She pinned it with her shoe, and was about to ease down to pick it up when she made the horrendous mistake of looking down at the street.

Bad move.

Her head swam with vertigo, her stomach heaved and the world veered crazily. Panicked that she was going to fall, with the hairs rising on her nape, she huddled to the wall and waited for the building to stop spinning, the fear and nausea to recede.

The world eventually righted itself, but she couldn't risk another move. She'd just have to stay there, frozen to the spot for the rest of her life.

Without the casement to cling to, her grip on the rough stone felt frighteningly tenuous. The window seemed miles away.

It dawned on her that she might not like heights. The ledge might have been nearly a metre wide, enough to support large pots of geraniums and whole generations of pigeons, but, three storeys from the Macquarie Street pavement, it seemed like a tightrope, a mere sliver of projecting stone.

The sky was darkening, the purple clouds making a rapid advance. She could feel the chill on the air as the temperature dropped. The wind buffeted her, her fingertips hurt and she all at once felt exhausted.

Tiny drops of rain on the wind stung her cheeks like grains of sand. How long would she last once it started properly? Already she was chilled to the bone, judging by her chattering teeth, although in some part of her brain she realised that was probably just the result of concentrated terror. But the force of the breeze in her face tired her and made her eyes water. She'd drop off the ledge soon with exhaustion. She imagined it on the news, the blazing headlines. WOMAN FALLS FROM LEDGE. CAT-WOMAN CAUGHT IN STORM.

How ironic. Killed by a change in the weather.

She realised with remorse that she hadn't spoken to Henry or Bea for a couple of months. Not since she'd contacted Elliott Fraser, in fact. What would they think when they heard? They'd be so hurt. She imagined them at the funeral, Bea weeping, Henry's face pinched with grief.

'Oh, my God.'

Connor's shocked exclamation broke through her musings from a great distance. She didn't dare turn her face towards him for fear of losing her balance and falling backwards.

After a moment he spoke to her. This time he sounded very calm. 'Sophy. Are you all right?' He was trying not to scare her, she realised dimly. 'Can you hear me?'

She had to strain against the wind to hear him, but there was no way she could risk the effort of replying.

He must have understood, because he said, 'Stay there. I'm going round to the other window.'

She supposed he felt furious. His tone, though, was merely brisk and capable. 'Stay quiet, don't jump and don't look down.'

Despite her fear, a measure of optimism revived. He must want to rescue her. And if he thought he could, then there must be some chance of her survival. There was hope. God. There was still hope.

After what seemed like an age but was probably a few seconds, she heard her own window open. She saw him lean out and lift a geranium pot inside, shift another one along out of the way. Then he tested his weight on the ledge, placed a foot on it so he was half in, half out, and stretched his hand out to her. She only needed to move a little way to be within touching distance, but her limbs were stuck in a sort of paralysis, in fear of letting go of this one safe spot.

Tying her heartstrings in knots, Connor didn't look furious, or mocking. His expression was calm and focused, the lines of his sexy mouth composed. Anyone would have thought he rescued daredevils from life-threatening situations every day of the week. The haven of his big body beckoned, exuding such solid competence, such safety and security, it seemed silly not to just throw herself into his arms at once.

If she hadn't already, in the most shaming way.

'Come on,' he cajoled, his deep, quiet voice confident and persuasive, as if he understood her fears exactly and sympathised. 'Just a little step further. You can do it.' His eyes were so warm and compelling, so trustworthy, her feet stirred into life and edged along an inch, halting abruptly as a sudden wind gust threatened to blow her into the street.

To her extreme relief, Connor repositioned himself, then managed to reach out far enough to grab her. His strong, warm hand closed around her arm. 'There, I've got you. Don't worry about the wind, just keep moving towards me. I won't let you fall. Trust me.' His eyes were so urgent and compelling, his deep, soothing voice so earnest and sincere, every fibre of her being wanted to be there with him. 'I won't let you fall,' he kept repeating. 'Come on, sweetheart. Come on.' His powerful frame, his open arms looked so warm and secure and inviting.

Sweetheart. In the exigency of the moment she pushed aside her wounded pride over the matter of the beach. Nothing mattered for the moment except for his dark eyes and his deep, mesmerising voice. The indignity of being wrapped safe in his strong arms would be better than trembling on a ledge for the rest of her life in a storm. She edged an inch towards him, hardly aware of the drag of her fingers on the rough sandstone.

'Come on. Just another step.'

She shuffled sideways. When she was close enough, he knelt back on her desk, which he'd shoved up against the window, and gripped her waist with sure, firm hands.

'Got you.'

As he helped her climb over the sill one of her shoes slipped off and disappeared.

'My shoe,' she cried, twisting round to see where it went.

Connor O'Brien didn't waste any time soothing her shattered nerves. 'Forget your shoe,' he said tersely, lifting her down to the floor with him and holding her against him so fiercely that mega-bolts of electric vibrations poured from his big, angry body into hers, and made her tremble all over like a willow frond.

But he felt so safe and solid and smelt so wonderfully male, being pressed furiously against him hardly seemed like punishment.

'I'm sorry for being a nuisance,' she whispered into his neck. 'Thanks for saving my life.'

Her abject apology only seemed to inflame him. He held her tightly to his chest for a further minute while the steam gathered, then released her as if she were an explosive device. Even though her legs felt like jelly, and she had to grab at her desk to support her-self, her body sang with the sensual textures of the contact with his hands and clothes and hard-muscled body.

The muscles in his face worked with the need to say something. She didn't need to do a clinical assessment to realise he was having a temporary word-finding problem.

At last he got some together. '*Look* at you.' He raked her with his ferocious gaze, shaking his head in incredulity. 'You're a mess. What the hell did you think you were doing?'

She clung weakly to the desk. She wished he'd stop yelling. As if she'd wanted to freeze with fear on the ledge. 'It was too narrow,' she explained, conscious of a bone-deep fatigue. 'It looked all right until I got on there and moved away from the window.'

His eyes flashed. 'I find it hard to believe an intelligent person could have done anything so stupid. Look at your hands.' He seized them.

She looked down and saw her fingers, grazed from the sandstone, the skin broken in some places. His hands were strong and lean, brown against her pale skin. It felt so good, so comforting, having her hands held, she wished he'd just go on holding them, but he dropped them in disgust to pace the room, flinging his arms about while he thundered.

'I can't for the life of me believe… What possessed you? That ledge is by no means secure. Bits of it are crumbling—*crumbling*, for God's sake—all around the building.' He paused to draw breath, his lean, handsome face taut, his mouth even more sensual and stirring than usual, set as it was in such severe lines. 'One minute you were there inside, safe and sound, the next you were…' He shook his head.

'It was the wind. It blew the letter outside and I was trying to retrieve it.'

He stared at her in thunderstruck incredulity. 'We are three storeys above the ground. Is a scrap of paper so important you'd risk your life?'

'I didn't think I *was* risking my life. I told you. The ledge looked…'

Did she really need to explain? She began to feel nauseous, and strangely detached from herself. She put her hand on his sleeve. 'Connor, I might need to sit down.'

She backed into a hard chair and sat down. For a while the world looked a bit woozy.

'Sophy.' Connor's face materialised and she saw he was kneeling before her chair, the lines of his face taut with concern. Remorse flickered in his eyes, and something else that made her shut hers quickly. 'Are you all right?'

'I could do with a drink.' Her voice was croaky, as if her throat needed lubricating.

He sprang up and came back with a glass of water, watching as she took it and drank. 'Thanks.' She handed back the glass.

She made a move to stand but he restrained her with a hand on her shoulder. 'Steady,' he warned, then gave a rueful sigh. 'Sorry. I shouldn't have been so… You're in shock. Stay quiet for a while. I thought you were about to keel over.' His voice rasped a little, and she realised he was in shock himself. 'What you really need is brandy.' He placed a gentle hand on her arm. 'God. You're as cold as ice.'

Her skin cells roused to his touch and she moved her arm away. He lowered his black lashes as turbulent memories stirred.

'I'm all right now.' She scrambled to her feet, ignoring her unsteady head, and the world swayed horribly. 'I'm fine.'

'The way you look, I find that hard to believe.' He steered her into an armchair, then took off his jacket and slung it around her shoulders. He gestured towards the door. 'Is there any kind of staff-room in there?'

She indicated and he went away, then returned in a few minutes with hot tea.

As she took the cup he murmured, shaking his head as he surveyed her torn fingers, 'Where's a doctor when you need one?'

'Who needs one? Just because I needed a little rest? I missed lunch today, that's all. All I want now is a good soak in a hot bath and a piece of toast.'

She supposed it was her weakened state, but the dark velvet eyes scrutinising her were so warm and concerned, not at all like the furious Connor O'Brien's of a moment ago, that in a rush of tremulous emotion she forgave him everything. Well, nearly everything. For smiling at Cindy, at least. Although, if he were married, she couldn't possibly forgive him that.

She sipped the tea without complaint, though it was a little on the strong side and had sugar in it. The truth was, it felt wonderful being pampered. Perhaps she should have thought of dancing on the ledge before. Just remembering it, though, must have been a mistake, for the world swam threateningly again.

Connor, keeping a watchful eye, immediately noted her change in colour. Experience told him that the overbright spark in her eyes would be shortlived and she would soon need to sleep. Still, something was nagging at him.

He said casually, 'You know, er…some people who weren't aware of your obsession with that letter might have wondered if you were planning to jump.'

'What people?' She rolled her eyes. 'Idiots? If I'd wanted to jump, don't you think I'd have picked something higher? Do you think I want injuries?'

He felt reassured enough to go back to his office to lock up. That small worry subsided, at least. Sure, her face had more colour since the near faint, but it was a tenuous improvement. She was still white with exhaustion, the shadow under her eyes now purplish hollows.

She might not have been planning to jump, but she needed some sort of attention. A hospital waiting room with its lacklustre service would hardly be useful. He remembered then with quick relief that both her housemates were nurses. Excellent. She could go home safely enough. He should be able to drop her at her door and make a clean getaway. Although…

He hoped they were reliable.

For God's sake, it was none of his concern. It was just that he knew too much about the aftermath of a crisis. Friends might bathe her wounds perhaps, but there was the night to come. Too well he knew the horrors waiting to torment the small hours after a near-death experience. He grimaced, and a dangerous thought flashed in.

Who would hold her through the night?

With a mental shake he brushed the temptation aside.

Finished locking up, he strode back into the clinic, and frowned to see her up and struggling to lift the potted geranium off the table.

'Hey, give me that,' he growled, snatching the pot from her and setting it down. He turned to her for a swift examination. She looked fragile, her exhaustion apparent, and he felt remorseful for the time he'd taken next door. 'It's time I got you home.'

Reading his glance, Sophy remembered what a wreck she must look. Her hair was a mess, she couldn't stop trembling, her hands hurt—she couldn't wait to escape from his sight and clean herself up.

She slung the strap of her bag onto her shoulder and held his jacket out to him.

'Thanks for your help.' She spoke stiffly, trying to stop her teeth from chattering. 'I'd better hurry now if I want to catch the ferry before the storm breaks.'

His brows shot up. 'The ferry! I don't think so.'

In all honesty, she did feel as if she were at the end of her strength, but she still had some pride. He'd been helpful—too helpful, really, for a man who'd made his position on involvements clear. The next thing she knew he'd be turning on her again the way he had at the beach. With as much dignity as any woman could be expected to muster without having shoes on both feet, she asserted, 'The ferry will be fine. All I need is a soak in a long, hot bath with some essential oils.'

For just the tiniest fraction of an instant he hesitated, then shook his head and started to make vigorous objections. But the protest came too late. Whatever he said now, she knew his first reaction had been relief. Relief at the notion of getting rid of her. She made a dignified attempt to move around him towards the door, but her uneven feet stumbled and she bumped into him.

He caught her arm. 'I'll drive you to the ferry.'

'No, no. You have your own concerns. I don't want you to put yourself out. There's absolutely no need for you to involve yourself any—'

His lips thinned. 'Pride isn't your most sensible option right now, Sophy.'

She froze for a second, then allowed herself to relent. 'Well, all right, then. Thanks. That would be quite—very generous of you.'

He paused to wait for her while she locked the clinic's outer door. In the gallery he had to slow his stride to match her limping gait. In the end she took off her one shoe and went barefoot, though it still felt like the longest mile she'd ever walked.

Waiting for the lift, he stood in brooding silence, then on the ride down, as she sagged, grateful for the wall, he said suddenly, 'I'll drive you all the way home.'

'Oh, heavens.' Her voice was faint with the effort of talking. 'There's no need for that. What's a bit of rain?'

His lips compressed, but all the walking must truly have worn her out, because when they stepped out into the basement car park, and she'd put her shoe on again to protect at least one foot from the greasy surface, Connor turned to her with an exasperated sigh and said, 'Oh, look. Here, hold this.' Before she had time to react, he thrust his briefcase into her grasp, wrapped his jacket around her and hoisted her up in his arms.

She gasped and stiffened, trying to control her overwhelming sensory response.

'What do you think you're doing?' she cried in a suffocated voice, conscious of his warm chest through the fabric of his shirt, his gorgeous mouth and masculine jaw, dark with five-o'clock shadow, close enough to graze her forehead. 'I *can* walk. There's no need for this—this—'

'I'm in a hurry,' he said curtly.

She knew she should have protested more strenuously. If the Avengers had been lurking in the car park, she knew they'd have swarmed over and wrested her from his arms and shrieked, 'For God's sake, Woodruff, stand on your own two feet and act like a *woman*.'

But, to be honest, it was fabulous to be in his arms, even so temporarily, and under what was clearly, for him, duress. Though he avoided looking down at her, he felt so strong and comfortable, and the close proximity of his hard, vibrant masculinity sparked up her flagging blood better than any swig of brandy could have done. While she might have still been feeling woozy, she savoured every second.

Then she let him swaddle her in the luxury of his big car and float her across the Harbour Bridge.

Darkness had descended. There were intermittent lightning flashes around the rim of the horizon, and the air felt heavy and expectant, as if the storm had made up its mind at last and was awaiting its moment to blow the sky apart.

Or maybe it was in the vibrations in the car. Even when she wasn't looking at Connor O'Brien, she was so tangibly aware of him, a few centimetres away from her.

They were nearly all the way to her place when he said, 'Will your friends be in this evening?'

'No.' She sighed. 'It's just me at the moment. They've gone on a camping holiday to Kakadu.'

He fell silent, his black brows heavy with thought. Suddenly he slowed, swung the car into a side street and pulled over. He turned his dark gaze on her. 'Look, I really don't think you should be alone tonight. You're in shock. Is there someone you can stay with?'

She shrugged. 'Millie, I suppose, only she lives at Penrith.' She wrinkled her brow. 'I'm not sure she'll be at home, though. They go out on Friday nights.'

'What about Fraser?'

'Who?' She stared at him aghast. 'Elliott Fraser? Are you serious? I hardly *know* him. He's a—a stranger. He doesn't even *like* me.' She became agitated, in her distress breathing very fast. 'For goodness' sake, Connor, just drop me at home, will you? I told you I'll be fine.'

He gripped the wheel, staring ahead into the night as though he were locked in battle with some inner demon. At long last, just when she was considering getting out to walk, he gave a long, fatalistic sigh, and muttered, 'No one could accuse me of not trying.'

Then he turned to look at her, and his posture relaxed a little. He started the car, swerved it into a neat U-turn, and headed straight back into the city.

She looked about her in alarm, afraid he was going to do something absurd like dump her in some hospital emergency room. 'Now what? Where…? Where are we going?'

'My place,' he growled.

His profile was grim, his stern, sexy mouth resolute. Normally she'd have been agog to visit his place of residence. Face it, hardly anything could have been more fascinating. She could find out for sure if he had a wife there, for one thing.

It only went to prove how shaken up she must have been by the ledge experience, that, although it was quite a short journey, she actually dozed off on the way. She only started from her stupor when she felt the car slow and make a sharp turn. They were driving along a tree-lined street in one of those wealthy suburbs. On either side, the lights of multi-level mansions glimmered richly behind high hedges and walls. There were some grand apartment buildings, with expensive cars parked in front. Above the rooftops on the lower side she could see the city lights.

'Wow,' she exclaimed, blinking, 'I can see the city. This looks very… Isn't this Double Bay?'

He drove them right to the end of the street. 'Point Piper,' he said, swinging the car into a gravelled drive.

Point Piper. Higher up the market than Double Bay. Only the most expensive real estate in Australia, home of bankers, billionaires and filthy rich property tycoons. At the end of the drive, right on the very point of the Point, they came to a pale, thirties-looking villa with rounded edges and three levels of balconies. No lights showed in its perfectly round windows. In the dark, it reminded her of a cruise liner with portholes. A ghost ship.

A garage door slid silently open, and automatic lights snapped on as they drove in. Connor O'Brien stood by while she got out of the car, and took her arm to steer her to the lift.

Normally, when given a choice, she preferred to bound up flights of stairs, but on this occasion she felt grateful the people in Point Piper had lifts in their car parks. Once inside the lift, though, the space seemed very small. Connor leaned against the opposite wall, flicking her the occasional smouldering glance from beneath his black brows. There was a tension in his lean frame that communicated itself to her with a skittery, jumpy excitement.

She noticed him loosen his collar and yank his tie free. Even in her weakened condition it was impossible not to appreciate how, with his tie undone and the dark shadow roughening his moustache and jaw, his quality of brooding sexiness seemed intensified.

'Maybe I should have just gone home to my place,' she said, her cool slipping a little.

His eyes glinted. 'Does your place have brandy?'

She admitted the lack of alcohol with a shrug.

'Look on the bright side.' He gave a low, sexy laugh. 'At least to-night there's no moon.'

She lowered her lashes. It was clear what he was worried about. He was afraid she might take advantage of the situation and throw herself at him again like a ravenous, sexually voracious virago. As if she could, in her state. Although, if she were forced to drink brandy...

The lift opened to a foyer with a parquet floor, and Connor O'Brien stood back to allow her entry.

She crossed the threshold, into his domain.

CHAPTER NINE

CONNOR reached for a switch and a soft light illuminated the bare foyer. As he ushered Sophy forward into a dim, cavernous space his arm brushed hers and her skin thrilled to the contact.

She was in a large empty room that flowed to other shadowy spaces. The effect of vastness was enhanced by high ceilings and wide windows. Through the glass she could see harbour lights blinking beneath the troubled sky. The place looked deserted.

One thing was certain. No wife lived here.

'What happened to your furniture?' Her voice echoed in the gloom. 'Have you been robbed?'

'No. Sit down and I'll get you a drink.'

'Where?' She peered into the shadows. 'Where do your guests sit?'

'Oh, er...' He hesitated, and glanced about in mild surprise as if he'd only just noticed the lack of the home comforts. She was looking down at the floor, thinking that would have to do, when he said, 'Come this way. Through here.' He led her through another dim room and paused to flick a switch.

A kitchen materialised in the light. It was spacious, with heavy, old-fashioned benches and a floor of chequered tiles. There was a grand old gas stove side by side with some more modern appliances. A sturdy kitchen table in the centre of the room looked as if it had seen long service, and there were a couple of high-backed chairs. There was a graceful long-legged stool at the wide counter, and she slipped onto it. Connor opened his fridge and peered inside. From where she sat the fridge was a repository of wide-open spaces. He gave a shrug, then went in search of his first-aid kit and the brandy.

'You're not married, then, Connor?' she said when he came back, as offhand as she knew how to be.

His hand paused in the act of pouring, and he sent her a deep glance. Of course he knew she'd seen that photo. 'Not currently.'

'But you were.'

'I was, yes,' he said easily. 'They—that picture you saw was of my wife and son. They were in a plane that crashed into a mountainside several years ago. In Syria.'

'Oh.' The appalling tragedy sucked the wind from her lungs. What was there to say? 'I'm so sorry. That's—that's truly terrible. You must have been through a dreadful time.' She flushed at the inadequacy of the words. 'I wish I could say—say *something*…'

He dropped his gaze. 'Don't worry, Sophy. There's nothing anyone can say. Here.' He handed her the glass with a warning murmur, 'Take it easy now.'

She took a bigger sip than she meant to, then coughed as her lungs seized and the liquid burned her throat. Connor poured himself a shot and leaned on his side of the counter, watching her recover herself with a wry expression.

'Do you ever take anything carefully?'

'Of course,' she gasped through watery eyes. 'I'm normally a very cautious person.'

'That's not my experience.' The warmth in his amused dark gaze was a dangerous temptation, playing on her longing, inviting her to drop her guard. On the other hand, surely there were moments between men and women when they should be able to come clean? But how was she to guess when it was safe?

'Well…' She traced her name in the dust on the counter.

'Lately…since I've known you, in fact…I've had—some exceptional circumstances.'

'What circumstances?'

'Well, there've been—things. Millie's move from next door. And then you… The things *you've* done…' She saw his brows shoot up and her heart skidded in dismay as she realised she was flirting with disaster. How close she'd come to spilling her guts and laying herself open to emotional slaughter. Leah and Zoe would have been horrified.

'Things.' He'd rolled his sleeves up to his elbows, and leaned lazily on his side of the counter, glass in hand, contemplating her. Doing it again. Charming her. Devastating her with his dark, velvet gaze. 'What sort of things? You mean, like making love to you?'

Her heart plunged and she turned her face quickly away. 'No, no,' she mumbled huskily. 'Not—that. I wasn't thinking of that at all.'

'Sophy.' He reached over and softly brushed her throat with his finger. 'This little pulse here tells me you're lying.'

Gentleness from a harsh man was so weakening. Her skin tingled where he touched, rivulets of fire in her willing flesh. She longed to respond to him honestly, but all the painful emotions of the beach churned up inside her and couldn't be denied. Did he think she could just carry on as though it had never happened?

She slid off the seat and headed for the blessed shadows of the empty sitting room. After a few tense moments he followed and reached for the light, but she stopped him. 'No, please,' she said, constraint in her voice. 'There'll be lightning soon. Let's—just enjoy it.'

The storm was building, but it wasn't the only reason she wanted to avoid the light. That casual little touch had roused the wildfire that resided in her blood for him, and thrown her into emotional uproar. The signals were all so conflicting. The things he'd said that night were seared into her brain, but the vibrations told a different story. Either he wanted her or he didn't. Or at least—somehow he wanted her, but at the same time he didn't.

It was a tightrope. She might as well have been back out on the ledge. Any false step and she could plummet straight to another debacle. And despite the strengthening prop of the brandy, she didn't think she was up to another one.

The night beat against the glass, pierced by the fretful lights of the marina, masts bobbing restlessly in the sullen dark.

Connor moved to stand beside her, wondering how he'd ever imagined it would be a simple matter to bridge the breach. How could he have forgotten the mysterious workings of the female mind? Now he could remember occasions with his wife when he'd been brought to a halt by that complexity. How had he managed then?

Of course. Sex. The great soother. But in the case of a *virgin*... Especially a virgin who'd been spurned by a damned fool...

He surveyed her tense profile. Instinct—dammit, every blood cell in his body prompted him to kiss her, unfasten that red dress and carry her straight to his bed. What else did a man do with a woman in an empty house? But he'd erected that barrier against himself.

He turned to her at the same instant as she turned to him. In the half-light the hollows and fatigue in her face made him piercingly aware of her fragility, despite the overbright sparkle in her eyes.

For God's sake, what sort of an animal was he? She'd just been through an ordeal. He couldn't just grab her and throw her on the bed.

'Have you ever seen *Last Tango in Paris*?' As soon as the words were out Connor closed his eyes, wincing at himself. Get a grip.

'I've heard of it. Was Marlon Brando in it?' He made a slight nod, and she added, 'What was it about?'

A man. A woman. An empty apartment.

Sophy heard his sudden hesitation and her insecurity increased. 'Look, Sophy...'

'This is such a fantastic house,' she exclaimed. 'I'd have expected it to belong to some billionaire.' Even to her own ears her voice sounded unnatural, echoing around the walls with nervous haste. Without giving him a chance to start again, she hastened to add, 'I don't mean to be rude, but is it that you can't afford furniture? Because I know some great little second-hand shops I could show you.'

He turned to examine her with an intent scrutiny, his black brows drawn. 'It's not that. This was my father's house for the last ten years of his life. Most of his stuff went to auction when he died.'

'So it's yours now?'

He gave a shrug.

Gosh. The O'Briens must be really up there. 'Your father wasn't that O'Brien who donated the wing to the children's hospital, was he?'

'That's right. I think he did do that. He was always very concerned about—charity.'

She nodded, trying to look nonchalant. 'Are you buying some furniture?'

'Haven't thought about it.'

'Er…don't you want to make it comfortable?'

'Is it uncomfortable?'

'Well, I was only thinking that if your friends come to visit…'

'You're the first.'

She was silent for a couple of heart-thuds. 'But what if your family…?'

'I don't have any more close family in Sydney. Just cousins and aunts I don't really know. No one even knows I'm here.' He smiled and his eyes gleamed with a seductive light. 'We have it all to ourselves.'

'Right.' Her heart started to thunder louder than the percussion section of the Sydney Symphony. She swallowed. 'Do you mind if I—look around?'

'Be my guest.'

She wandered from room to room and he followed, switching on lights for her. The rooms were nearly all empty, gracious bedrooms with wide windows looking onto the harbour and large, old-fashioned bathrooms. A staircase led to the upper storeys, but Connor admitted he never bothered to go up there unless he was scrounging for bits and pieces that had escaped the auctioneers.

There was one room with a desk and media equipment, as well as a new-looking leather armchair with a standard lamp, and she noticed a stereo and a pile of CDs in one corner. And there was his bedroom.

She stood poised at the door. The bed was large, necessary for a tall man, with side tables and a matching chest of drawers. It looked like the sort of furniture that could be bought from a warehouse catalogue, something you could phone up for and have delivered. But to her exhausted self it looked so inviting, all at once, with its deep red-and-gold covers, plump pillows with snowy white cases. She ached to plunge into its softness and surrender her aching limbs to its embrace.

Her glance fell on a suitcase on the floor. She stared at it for seconds.

Connor O'Brien was watching her, his eyes veiled as her eyes switched from suitcase to bed. 'Would you like to try it?'

'Oh, no, no, thanks.' She backed from the room.

'You should rest. Those shadows under your eyes are deeper.' He reached out to brush them lightly with his thumb. 'You've been through an ordeal.'

She lowered her lashes. 'It's all right. I'm fine now. I'll—phone for a taxi in a minute and go home.'

He was silent for a few seconds, his brows drawn. Then he shrugged and shoved his hands into his pockets. 'You don't have to phone for a taxi, Sophy. If you'd really prefer to go home I'll drive you.' After a second he added with a shimmering glance, 'You would be quite *comfortable* in that bed.'

She looked quickly at him. He looked grave, but had there been the hint of a smile in his voice? She wished she'd had a string of lovers and could read men's minds. What did he intend? If there was only one bed...

The stormy sky over Sydney Harbour mirrored her inner turbulence. The truth was, in recent days she'd have thought there was nowhere in the world she'd rather be than in an empty house with Connor O'Brien, but that had been when she thought she didn't have a chance. Now there seemed to be the glimmer of a possibility, she wasn't sure. After the last disaster, was it worth taking such a risk again? He couldn't just turn her on and turn her off when he felt like it. A woman had her pride.

On the other hand, she'd always felt very affected by storms. Perhaps the atmospheric disturbance had jammed her sexual sensors into the *On* position. He might, in fact, just be acting the Good Samaritan role. He'd already told her in the most devastating way that he didn't want an involvement. And if that wasn't enough, she'd just had the strongest possible cosmic flash.

This home was temporary.

He was going away.

It gave her such a hollow feeling. She wandered back to the shadows of the large room, Connor's thumbprint still on her face, a storm in her heart. Common sense told her she shouldn't be dreaming of him. Everyone knew it was easy for a man to make love to a woman, then just go away and forget her. But for the woman...

She supposed some women could take it in their stride. Shrug their shoulders and move on. Next, please, as Zoe always said. But in her case... In this case...

Moving on had never been her forte.

Outside the planet was holding its breath. Something was about to break loose. The first fat drops of rain spattered against the glass.

Just when the suspense reached an unbearable pitch a jagged fork of lightning zigzagged across the sky and illuminated the room in greenish neon. For a second she saw Connor's tall, solitary frame, outlined in the gloom of his empty house. A moment later a deafening crack of thunder split the air, making the windows rattle. He brushed past her to close the blinds and she felt the shock of contact with his bare forearm.

Silence reclaimed the room before the next onslaught and all she could hear was her pounding heart, the throb of her blood, or was it his?

He turned to her, his eyes burning with a dark flame in the half-light. For a breathless second she waited, yearningly aware of every part of him—the rise and fall of his chest, the masculine hairs curling on his long limbs, his heart beating its dark, mysterious rhythm. If he took her in his arms now, she wouldn't be phoning for any cab.

He reached out and smoothed his fingers over her left cheekbone. 'You've got a little graze here.' His voice sounded as deep as a gravel pit. His fingers travelled further, tracing the line of her jaw, rousing light rays in her skin. 'You look gorgeous in that dress.'

His voice was so deep she held her breath, waiting for him to seize her and press his beautiful, sexy mouth to hers. But he dropped his hand and his eyes narrowed.

'Are you sure you're all right? You're looking a bit fragile. I really think you should rest. And you need food. Have a little sleep then we'll find you something to eat.'

A *sleep*. Was he kidding? How romantic. Next he'd be tucking her up in bed with a hot-water bottle and a tray with a boiled egg and soldiers.

If she had been a sophisticated woman of the world, she'd give him a breezy wave now and sashay to the door. The trouble was, the thought of sashaying fatigued her through to her very marrow.

A wave of exhaustion washed over her. She slid down the wall onto the floor and leaned back. 'I'll just have a little rest before I phone for the cab.'

Connor looked bemused. 'No. No, for God's sake, you can't sit there. Come and lie down on the bed.'

Gingerly, she lay down on her side. 'It's just for a minute.'

He lowered his lashes for a second, then his eyes glinted with rueful comprehension. 'You're—welcome to use the bed, Sophy.'

'I like the floor,' she lied. 'I often prefer the floor. I'll just close my eyes for a second before I phone...'

His sensuous mouth tightened. Frowning, he shook his head. 'It's not a good idea to travel in a storm. We really should be looking at bathing those wounds. You need to rest properly. I don't think I have any spiritual essences on hand, but there's plenty of soap and hot water here. Towels and—everything.'

The bath sounded tempting, but she was just too tired. She stretched out, the hard boards ruthlessly crunching her bones at shoulder, hip and ankle. 'Maybe.'

He stared fascinatedly down at her as she pillowed her head on her arms. 'I suppose I should do something about dinner.' His gaze flicked to her bare legs and feet and hung there as though mesmerised. 'I'll order some in. What do you feel like? Thai, Turkish, Indian, Chinese?'

'Oh, what do I know?' She sighed. 'Is that what you do every night? Order in takeaway?'

'What's wrong with takeaway?'

He stood there, hesitating, then dropped onto the floor a little way from her. It wasn't so very far. He could have reached across to take her in his arms if he'd wanted to. Every fibre of her flesh and blood yearned towards him. But he only said, 'Sophy…won't you tell me what's got you in such a bind over that letter? It isn't some sort of blackmail, is it?'

God. If she wasn't sick to death of that stupid letter. She was glad it was gone now for all time. She never wanted to lay eyes on it again.

She felt the last of the spurious energy drummed up by the brandy drain away. Surrendering to the inevitable, she tucked her hands under her cheek and closed her eyes, mumbling, 'It's my DNA profile.'

She let herself drift. She stopped noticing the boards pressing into her, as if they'd developed grooves in the right places. After what seemed like an age she was floating, floating down that river towards a beckoning golden shore when she felt a strong arm, gentle and sure under her shoulders, another under her knees, and knew Connor O'Brien was lifting her off the floor.

CHAPTER TEN

SOPHY surfaced to the sound of clattering dishes. Smells tickled her nostrils, delicious cooking smells, and her stomach groaned. She was in a bed. It gradually homed in on her that it could only be Connor's. She opened her eyes. Sure enough, she was in a strange room and she could hear the comfortable sound of rain outside. She woke a little further and stretched with luxurious relish. Somehow Connor's mattress supported and massaged her every aching muscle. She spread out her arms and made a voluptuous little shimmy, soaking up every molecule of the personal O'Brien essence while she had the chance. A quick bodily survey made her realise she felt rested and alive.

Her optimism level made a surprising upward bound. It was amazing how invigorating a nap in his bed could be.

'Good. You're awake.'

She started and blinked as a soft light illuminated the room. Her eyes focused, then refocused on Connor standing at the door. Her insides curled over and she sat up. He'd changed into jeans and a dark casual T-shirt that outlined the athletic contours of his lean body. His hair glistened as if it was damp, and she wondered if he'd shaved, he looked so fresh and scrubbed and relaxed. And handsome, she thought, her heart surging. It wasn't fair. It just wasn't fair that a man should be so… She noticed his gleaming, dark gaze riveted to her in the bed.

Aware suddenly of her dress rucked up around her thighs, she scrambled to draw the tangled covers up to her waist and sat up.

'How long have I been asleep?' Knowing she must look all flushed and tousled, she made an attempt to smooth her hair.

'A couple of hours.'

His voice had thickened slightly as his gaze drifted below her chin. Glancing down, she saw her bodice twisted askew, drawn too tightly over her breasts, and made a hurried attempt to fix it.

'Are you hungry?'

'I am,' she said, her own voice nearly as husky. 'Ravenous, you might say.'

His lashes flickered and she saw the corners of his sexy mouth edge up. 'Good. I dropped down to the night market and picked up a few things for dinner.' He angled away, leaning his weight on one foot. 'Would you like me to—run you a bath?'

Had she died and gone to heaven?

As soon as he left she scrambled out of the bed, smoothed and straightened it back to its neat beginnings.

The old-fashioned bathroom was an indulgence of ornate mirrors and white marble surfaces, with that last word in roaring twenties-style decadence, a sunken bath. While she stood admiring it, Connor produced a comprehensive first-aid kit.

'What are they for?' she enquired, noticing a couple of lethal-looking clinical tools like tweezers, with little lights attached.

'Oh, you know.' He pushed in the little drawer in the kit that held them. 'Picking up things, small particles caught in your skin, etc.'

'Bullets.' The word whizzed into her head and popped out before she even connected with it.

His startled gaze flew to meet hers, then almost at once his eyes veiled and he said lightly, 'You know, you're a worry, with that imagination of yours.'

She kept reminding herself, as he moved the conversation on, giving her instructions about antiseptic and adhesive tape, showing her where the towels were stored—his two spare towels—that he might be very hospitable, but nothing else had changed. He was still a man who had some very mysterious layers. And he had rejected her on a beach.

'Anything else? Need to know where anything is?'

She screwed up her face. 'I just wish I had some clean clothes to change into.'

'Can't help you there. Unless…' He hesitated, then his face smoothed to become expressionless. 'I suppose you could try one of my shirts.'

The bathroom space suddenly shrank to the size of a cupboard. She avoided his eyes. Surely wearing something of his would be a dangerously intimate move. And then there was the problem of undies.

'I don't know,' she mumbled. 'I'll think about it.'

After a fraught two seconds he strode out and returned with a clean blue shirt on a laundry hanger, which he hung on the door. 'My last offer. Take it or leave it.'

As the voluptuous sunken bath filled and the steam rose, and the moment for him to withdraw from the room with gentlemanly grace approached, it occurred to her with a leap in her pulse that Connor was not altogether impervious to her charms.

There was still hope. There was always hope.

'Oh, and I forgot,' he said gruffly. 'This was all they had at the market.'

He thrust a package into her hands. Mystified, she ripped off the brown chemist paper and widened her eyes in astonishment. Oils. He'd brought her essential oils.

'Oh, my God.' Overcome, she blinked and shook her head. 'Connor! *Well*, this is just… This is *so*… So very *thoughtful*…'

'I'll leave you to it,' he said brusquely, removing himself. 'Don't be long.'

If the sleep had been invigorating, the bath was blissful. She lay back in the water, redolent of rosemary and clary sage, and let the soothing essences permeate her spirit with their healing power, while she considered Connor O'Brien. Could she be dreaming? Had the sense of emergency pervading the evening since her rescue changed something between them? Soon though, driven by hunger pangs, she rose and towelled herself dry until she tingled and her skin felt silky soft.

She tried on the shirt. It nearly came down to her knees front and back, although not at the sides. She considered the degree of thigh exposure, but, when she'd turned back the cuffs about twenty times, decided it was no less modest than most things. It just *looked* suggestive.

Connor seemed to think so, anyway, when she finally met him in the kitchen. He glanced up from stirring a saucepan on the stove. Instantly the hand that held the spoon stilled and his eyes flared with that hot, sensual gleam that made her nipples harden with yearning.

'Ah,' he said softly. 'You look much better. More like your old self.'

More like the old self of his fantasy, Connor thought, his heart rate escalating in erotic appreciation of the shirt hanging from her slim shoulders with surprising elegance. *His* shirt grazing *her* nipples.

There was only a glimpse of cleavage. If only he hadn't had such a good memory.

He poured her a glass of red wine with a steady hand, though his blood buzzed with every angle of thigh revealed and concealed by the shirt's uneven hem.

He clinked glasses with her, smiling, forcing his eyes not to drift below her chin. If she hadn't been a virgin, he might have trailed his hand up that smooth thigh and under the shirt. He turned sharply back to the stove, his jeans all at once tight.

Sophy perched on the stool and sipped her wine very sparingly. There was something very sexy about Connor's cooking style. He tasted his brew, threw in extra salt, slapped on the lid, stooped to check on something aromatic he was heating in the oven, his movements all with a swift, casual grace that was so essentially masculine.

At the same time her excitable senses attuned to a silent conversation pulsing in the air between them, drumming with the rain, underlying every spoken word and glance.

When he set her soup before her, the fragrant steam rising from it sent her weak at the knees. Or perhaps it was the wine infusing her bloodstream. Or him.

'Bon appetit,' he murmured.

The meal had an Eastern theme. There was tabouleh salad he'd bought from a deli, delicious little kofta meatballs with pine nuts, and flatbread with hummus. More than enough for a late-night supper, marooned on a rainy night in an empty house with a sexy, dark-eyed man.

After her last spoonful, she exclaimed, 'Delicious.'

And it had been. Lentils and spinach, lemon and coriander, cumin and some other Eastern spice. Heavenly nourishment for her grateful stomach.

'Have some more,' he urged. 'You need to build up your strength.'

'That's very good of you, Connor, but I can't fit any more in. I'm so impressed you went to the trouble of cooking. And such an exotic soup. Who'd have thought you'd be so domesticated?'

He smiled. 'It's one of the few things I can cook. It's a very common, ordinary dish in the Middle East.'

'Oh, of course. You were in Iraq.'

'You should know.' He made a wry grimace. 'After all your snooping around my office I've started to wonder if you're a detective.'

She smiled. 'Snooping. Now, there's an overstatement. I may, perhaps, have accidentally come across your passport while conducting my own affairs…'

'Ah, yes. Your affairs. I think that's what we should be talking about.' His dark eyes were gentle and teasing, piercingly sensual.

'I don't think so. Tell me more about Iraq. Did you live at the embassy?'

'Some of the time. Sometimes I travelled to other places.'

'It must have been terribly dangerous.'

The lean, tanned hands resting on the table curled, but he said evenly, 'Everywhere is dangerous. Nowhere more so than the Alexandra in Sydney.'

'Oh, now how is that dangerous?'

He said softly, a smile edging up the corners of his mouth, 'There are traps there for the unwary. Beautiful, lethal temptations.'

Adrenaline rushed along her veins like a torrent of the warm red wine.

'You mean, those danishes in the coffee shop? They *are* very appetising.' She leaned her elbows on the table and rested her chin in her hands. 'When are you going back?'

His eyes registered a hit, but veiled almost at once. 'Who said I was—' He broke off. 'Never mind that now. There's something I think we need to straighten out.'

She slumped back in her chair and heaved a sigh. 'Right. The letter, I suppose.'

'No, not the letter. I can guess what that's about.' He frowned down at the table for a few seconds, his forehead creased in seriousness, then reached across and took her hands with such an earnest expression that her insides clenched in anxiety. 'I—I've been wanting to say something to you. I'm not very good at this, but… You know that night at the beach… I shouldn't have… I—know I hurt your feelings. It's on my conscience. I'm sorry, Sophy. You didn't deserve that. I apologise.'

There was sincerity in his gaze and she felt herself flush. She knew she'd reached another seminal moment. But it was hard to bear him touching that sore spot, however carefully. Her heart was racing for gold, but it was time to stand up tall and act like a woman. Thank God for adrenaline.

'What feelings, Connor?' She flexed her hands in his strong, warm grasp so that her fingers laced through his. 'I'm a big girl. Isn't it time we left all that behind us and moved on? Now, what's for dessert?'

Connor's grip on her hands tightened. The sensual flame in his dark eyes intensified, and he said softly, 'Don't you know?'

His hands slid to her upper arms, and he leaned across and took her mouth in a searing kiss. Some dishes clattered at their elbows, but he seemed oblivious of them. He pulled her up out of her chair, still kissing her, and drew her away from the table into his arms, pressing her soft curves against his hard, angular frame.

She responded with all she had, and he deepened the kiss to a sizzling, sexual intensity, his tongue darting in to plunder her mouth. As the heady flavours of wine, lemon and him invaded her senses, her bones dissolved and she had to cling to his shoulders for support.

As his hands sought her breasts through the shirt, and slid down to her hips and thighs, her blood ignited with a heavy, pulsing turbulence like a fever, and she wanted to hold him, and experience him with every inch of her skin.

His erection nudged hard against her belly, and, unaccountably, a small rush of moisture pooled between her legs.

The kiss grew frantic, and when she was out of breath and drowning, he broke away from her, his powerful chest rising and falling.

'Is this what you want?' he said hoarsely.

She nodded, wondering if she hadn't given clear enough womanly signals. She took a step in the direction of the bedroom, glancing back to draw him after her with her eyes, but he didn't need any encouragement. He just swept her up in his arms. He'd done it before, but this time it was so thrilling, and romantic, and as he strode along with her, she reached up for another burning taste of his mouth.

He laid her on his bed, and stood gazing at her for a few moments, his eyes blazing like hot coals while she waited, barely breathing, excitement gathering in her like a storm. Then he sat on the edge of the bed and took off his shoes.

She hoped he wasn't getting cold feet again.

'I've got some condoms in my bag if you need any,' she said in an offhand tone.

He broke into a grin. 'Have you, now?' Then he grew grave, though his eyes glowed with tender amusement. 'Well, as it happens, I have some on hand. But if we need any more, we'll use yours.'

He opened the drawer in the bedside table, pulled out a handful, and laid them on the pillow. Her shirt had ridden up a little, and to her surprise he tugged at the edge of it to pull it down more demurely.

What the...? He *did* know what he was doing?

'So...' she breathed, 'what happens now?'

He stretched out beside her on the bed, leaning up on his elbow and gazing down at her, a flame behind the sultry smile in his eyes. 'Well, now. First, we have a little kiss.' He held her jaw lightly while he kissed her mouth, then he pressed his scorching lips in little feathery kisses across her eyebrows, cheeks and jaw. When he reached her throat, the heat of the kisses intensified, and she could feel her breasts swell with arousal and longing.

'Would you like to take off my shirt?' she panted, her voice husky.

His eyes shimmered. 'What do you have under it?'

She hadn't read hundreds of *Cosmo* articles for nothing. 'Isn't that for you to find out?'

He seemed to thrive on the challenge. He changed position, switching his attention to her feet. He lifted the right one in his hand, rubbed his thumb over the sole, and bent his dark head for a long, caressing kiss into the hollow of her ankle.

Oh, God. It was so *seductive*. Little rivers of tingling delight rayed through her foot and somehow settled in the lower regions of her abdomen. Who'd have thought feet and ankles could be so erogenous?

She sank deeper into the bed. 'The other one, Connor. *Please.*'

He obliged, this time with an even more sensual assault on her ankle, appraising her face with shimmering eyes. She was still thrilling as his lean, supple hand edged further up her legs, caressing them as if they were made of satin. When he reached her knees, he smoothed his hand over them as if their rounded shape gave him intense, sensual satisfaction. The more he stroked her, the more his hand seemed increasingly charged with some high-voltage current that radiated straight to her interior. While his eyes…

His eyes held her mesmerised. As his caresses travelled up her thigh, his hot, lustful gaze set her throbbing with a heavy, yearning pulse.

He was so cunning. Fire dripped from his fingers. His hand slid up under the shirt hem, stroking the soft skin of her upper thigh with a sensual intent that made her tremble with suspense.

'Aha,' he said, connecting with the elastic hem of her pants and giving it a playful tug. Then, just as she braced in expectation of him slipping them off, he slid his hand down to the inside of her thigh, just above her knee. She tensed, barely breathing, then he bent suddenly, and with his tongue traced an electric path along the silken skin, nearer and nearer to the flimsy fabric that hid her tingling, throbbing secret place.

Her mouth dried in anticipation. But just before he made the crucial connection he paused and raised his head, a wickedness in his eyes. 'Let's take that shirt off now.'

Now? She wanted it off, of course, it was making her so *hot*, but…

He sat up and pulled off his T-shirt. In the soft light his wide chest was satin bronze, the dusky hairs curling up on it an irresistible temptation. The scar at his ribs stood out in startling contrast, and she reached out to smooth her fingers over it, but he held her hand still. 'No.'

He stretched out on his side, leaning languidly up on one elbow, gazing at her with such sinful intent in his dark, slumbrous gaze that her insides turned to liquid. His hand slid below the shirt to undo her top button, then beneath his black lashes she saw the flare in his eyes as he gazed on the swells of her breasts. One by one he released all the buttons, so that the shirt edges separated. With a husky groan, he bent his burning lips to her breasts, cupping each one in his hand, stroking them until she nearly swooned with pleasure.

It was so fantastic and arousing, she couldn't resist moaning. Her breathing became increasingly hoarse and shallow. Then he trailed greedy little kisses of fire all the way to her navel, then on to the upper edge of her pants.

And there he paused.

But surely. Surely he would…

'Ah. Let's take that shirt all the way off.'

She sat up and he helped her off with the shirt. Then he gazed at her with a hot, intense gaze. She glanced self-consciously down at her breasts, wondering what he was thinking.

'Care to bite anything?'

His lustful face broke into a husky laugh, then he grabbed her in his arms and kissed her lips, tenderly at first, then with mounting fierceness. As his tongue ravished her mouth she could feel his big powerful heartbeat, thumping in electric communication with hers.

Her heart filled with emotion. She ached with everything in her to be close to him, as close as a human being could be to another person. Responding with fervour, she wound her arms around him and clung, aroused by the feel of his chest hair in friction with her breasts, craving for every form of contact as he pushed her down with him onto the bed.

He kissed her throat and breasts, and the yearning that was storming her blood set her every skin cell alight with erotic craving. Her nipples were so hard and aching, so throbbing with need for attention, that when he closed his mouth over first one, then the other and tenderly licked them with his tongue, *then* drew hard on them with his mouth, she nearly went wild.

'Oh, Connor,' she gasped, shuddering with pleasure as his passion moved on to rage over her prostrate body. Between her thighs, a searing hunger blazed, but his lips and devouring, inflammatory hands stopped short of that potent spot.

He leaned up for a second, motionless, watching her face.

She felt the air in the room tauten.

'What are we waiting for?' Her voice was nearly a croak.

He smiled, then all at once whipped her pants down to her ankles.

She heard the sudden quickening of his breath. 'You're—beautiful.' His voice was thick and unsteady. For her to have such a powerful effect on him filled her with thrilled wonder.

The room crackled with tension as he gazed at her nude body with rapt appreciation. But, in a sudden anxiety, she couldn't help thinking of the last time.

Swallowing, she ventured, 'Connor, you're not—you're not still worrying about me being a virgin, are you?'

For an instant his eyes closed. Then with a long, shuddering groan he bent his sensuous mouth to her soft nest of curls in a kiss more tender and arousing than she could ever have imagined. She made wild little gasping cries of sheer pleasure, parting her thighs for him, clenching and quivering as his lips and tongue flicked across the tender, yearning tissues. The sensation was so delicious, so exciting, she was in an ecstasy of wanton sexual rapture, until all too soon the erotic frenzy came to a halt. He paused, lifted his head to cast a long, smouldering glance at her, then rolled away.

He sprang off the bed and, without taking his eyes from her, unbuckled his belt and stripped off the rest of his clothes.

The breath caught in her throat at his power and beauty. He was so tall and strong and well made, the lines of his long, sinewy limbs and lean, muscled body as graceful and stirring as any classical sculpture. But when her gaze fastened on the robust length and thickness of his engorged penis, her eyes widened. For a second her courage nearly took a dive.

She tried not to show her momentary cowardice, but Connor's watchful gaze on her face was instantly aware.

'Sophy, Sophy.' He sat down on the bed beside her and kissed her lips very gently. Then he drew her hand to touch him. 'Feel the skin here,' he murmured. 'This is not designed to hurt you.'

She closed her hand around him, marvelling at the velvet texture of the skin encasing the rock-hard shaft, while he kept motionless, only a small tremor and the glitter in his eyes showing his effort of will not to react.

'Well,' she exclaimed. 'You are very... You're *very*... Who'd have guessed?'

A tinge of amusement crossed his face, but he gently removed her hand. Then he took her by her shoulders and laid her down. His smile slowly faded as his smouldering dark gaze feasted on her nude body with a fierce possessiveness that shook her.

He extracted a sheath from the packet on the pillow, and eased it onto his virile arousal as she lay motionless, pricking with anticipation, her breasts, her skin, every part of her aflame.

He turned to her and she whispered, 'So...?'

'So.' With one provocative finger he drew a line of fire in her sensitised skin from her collarbone to the apex of her thighs. Then he slipped his hand between her legs, parting them a little, and softly, with exquisite gentleness, stroked the tender, burning flesh until she moaned and gasped.

Then his clever fingers brushed the most aroused spot of all. 'Ah-h-h...'

He slipped a finger inside her, stroking her with patient concentration. Every part of her felt aflame with hunger, his every light touch was the most intense, searing pleasure.

Suddenly he paused, then rolled his big, lean body on top of hers, supporting his weight on his arms, and positioning himself between her parted legs.

She could feel the rapid beat of his heart, hear his heavy breathing as he contemplated her.

'Link your ankles behind my back,' he commanded.

She complied, and he gazed down at her, his eyes glowing with a dark flame. She felt the velvet tip of his hard penis nudge at her moist entrance, then he made a firm, insistent push.

She felt an uncomfortable pressure and dug her fingers into his shoulders, straining with tension.

'Easy now,' he ground out. 'Just relax.' Then he thrust again, a little more firmly.

This time she felt a sharp, raw tweak of her tender tissues. He was inside her, his face settling into an expression of absolute ecstatic triumph, while she clenched her entire body and cried, 'Hey.'

He froze, searching her face in alarm. Then he eased himself out of her, his eyes closing momentarily as if even the backwards movement was the most sublime pleasure.

'Are you all right?' His voice was a deep rasp. His brows drew together, and he said, breathing heavily, concern in his dark eyes, 'Are you hurting?'

She made a rapid review of her discomfort and realised she wasn't, not really, and made an effort to relax. 'Not now. It's all right.'

He still frowned, raking her face, and she said huskily, in an effort to tease, 'What do you think? Am I made of glass?'

He stroked the hair back from her hairline, his hand gentle and soothing, though unsteady, like his breathing. He grazed her cheekbone with his lips. 'We can stop if you want to.'

His dark eyes were so tender and at the same time so fierce and hot, a dark, heavy heat pooled deep inside her. 'No,' she whispered. 'Don't stop.'

His pupils darkened and he made a sharp little intake of breath, then bent his lips to hers in a deep, searing kiss. As her senses swam to the taste of him, the passion rose in her like a seething tide. With a little involuntary sound in her throat, she locked her legs around him.

He eased carefully into her, filling her, scanning her face with his hot, possessive gaze until she got used to the unusual feeling. Then he started a gentle rhythm of slow, controlled moves while she grew accustomed to the strange erotic pleasure, enjoying the curled hairs on his chest and legs brushing her smooth skin. With gradual care he increased the tempo, and her flesh ignited to the sexy rocking. Little streamlets of delight roused in her and spread like rays of the sun. She clung to his powerful, athletic body, arching and giving herself up to him, barely conscious of her own desperate, hoarse little cries.

As though hearing the fevered beat of her blood, Connor escalated the rhythm, thrusting faster and faster, until passion and pleasure entwined to propel her up a wild, exhilarating climb, higher and higher, to a peak where her wild, frenzied tension hung poised, then shattered and dissolved in a rapturous, blissful release.

His big, strong body bucked, and he emitted a deep groan that sounded as if it came from the very depths of him. He collapsed on top of her, and lay panting there for several seconds, his cheek against hers, while their bodies were slick with their efforts.

He rolled away from her, and after a time visited the bathroom. The dark felt soft and caressing on her skin as she lay there, listening to the running water, reviewing all the sensations of her body after her momentous initiation.

Connor returned and slipped into the bed beside her. He lay there silently for a while, his elbow crooked over his eyes. Eventually he roused himself and turned on his side to gaze at her, his dark eyes glowing into hers with such warmth she felt bathed in the light of the sun.

'Well, then, Sophy Woodruff?'

Smiling, she turned to face him. 'Well, then, Connor O'Brien.'

Softly he traced her silhouette with his finger, while her heart brimmed with a million tremulous, heartfelt things she needed to say to him. But he whispered, 'Shh, sweetheart,' kissed her lips, and pulled her close in against his big, warm body. 'Go to sleep.'

CHAPTER ELEVEN

BREAKFAST at Connor's was a casual affair. Sophy didn't have any clean clothes, so she was forced to stay in bed. At least, that was Connor's reasoning.

On first awakening, she gently disentangled herself from his embrace, and tiptoed to the bathroom. She borrowed his soap for a warm wash, cleaned her teeth with toothpaste on her finger, and, unable to locate her clothes, wrapped herself in a towel. When she emerged, Connor was lying awake, gazing out the window at the grey view of the harbour, dismal with misty rain. She hesitated at the door, uncertain of the etiquette. Wasn't it time to wave a sophisticated au revoir and saunter to the door?

Anyway, she had washing to do at home, her library books to return, and the house to clean before Zoe and Leah came back from their camping trip.

'Oh, good,' she said, a little breathless. 'You're awake. Do you know where my clothes are? I have some things I have to do at home. There's the—the housework, and...'

Connor turned to examine her, and leaned up on his elbow, as languid as a big, lazy panther. His dark, sinful gaze and the black growth of his beard gave him a villainous look.

'I have to...have to go to the library...'

He gave his brows a seductive lilt and lifted the bedcovers, patting the spot beside him.

Her bones dissolved. His bronzed chest with the dark whorls of hair looked so warm and inviting. With a surge of excitement she managed to walk primly back until the very last second, when she dropped the towel and dived, giggling, under the covers and into his arms.

At some later stage he got up and showered, leaving her body humming with pleasure and a certain amount of soreness, her heart in a state of thrilled suspension. Then somehow locating her clothes along with his own, he blew her a kiss and went out in his car.

What was a prisoner to do? She took the opportunity for a long, relaxing shower.

Connor returned with hot croissants, sour strawberry jam and double cream, lattes and golden peaches with rosy skins. 'I couldn't resist them,' he said, kissing her shoulder where the T-shirt he'd lent her kept slipping. 'They reminded me of you.'

The dearth of furniture was a blessing in some ways. On a rainy Saturday, the bed was the cosiest place for the breakfast feast.

It wasn't long before the conversation came around to her letter. Connor's quick brain had made the connection about her relationship with Elliott, of course. He kept shaking his head and saying, 'I should have realised at once.'

There was no point trying to conceal anything from him any longer, and she told him all of it, the meetings, the disastrous dinner at the hotel. She couldn't prevent her voice from wobbling a bit when she told him about Elliott's offer of money to buy her silence.

Connor looked grave. 'Not a very clever way to handle it. He must feel very threatened.'

She glanced quickly at him. 'I realise he must, of course. If he didn't know I even existed, then it's come as a terrible shock. Anyone would feel threatened. But it's funny, I have the strongest feeling he's lying to me about something. I wouldn't be a bit surprised if he *did* know. He knew that Sylvie—that was my mother—had died. Surely he would have known she left a child.'

'He might have known that, without knowing you were *his*

child.' He licked some croissant crumbs from where they'd landed on her thigh. 'That was a tragedy, your mother dying when you were so young.'

'It was,' she agreed, sighing. 'But I was so lucky, being adopted by the Woodruffs. They were wonderful parents, and so generous. You know, they haven't sold their house. They might still decide to come back.'

His brows knitted, and he scanned her face. 'That must have been hard for you when they left. How old were you?'

'Eighteen. It was hard at first, but I got over it. People have to move on and grow up, don't they? It did me good in some ways. Taught me to be independent. How many people move out of home at that age? It's really very normal.'

His eyes were pensive. 'How do they feel about your contacting Elliott?'

She lowered her lashes. 'Well, I haven't exactly mentioned it. To be honest, I doubt if they'll mind one way or the other.'

Connor frowned, considering. From all he'd heard, adoptive parents felt equally threatened when their children chose to search for their birth parents. And though it might be normal for people to leave home when they attained their adulthood, it wasn't all that normal for parents to be the ones who left the children. And the country. Such a total abandonment.

'Why did they go back to England?'

'Well, Bea has a daughter from an earlier marriage. She and her husband moved back to live in England. Lauren had some problems during her first pregnancy, so naturally Bea wanted to be with her. They only meant to visit for a few months at first. But the baby was born with some disabilities, so they decided to stay on to give Lauren support. And now other children have come along, and I think they love being grandparents. You know how it is. Blood is thicker than water, as they say. I guess that's why I feel so interested to know about my own parents.'

Connor felt a twinge. Could Sophy Woodruff truly feel so little bitterness about having been abandoned by two sets of parents, for whatever reasons?

He rubbed his jaw. 'It shouldn't be so hard to check up on all of it. Are you sure you want to go ahead? You might find out things you don't want to know.'

'I've considered that. Even if I discover that Elliott is not some-one I particularly like, there's little Matthew. I'd love to have a little brother. And, you know, I suspect Elliott isn't really very kind to him. That has a huge bearing on a child's development, you know. He needs people to talk to him, be interested in him.'

'There might be—other people in the family who do.'

'I hope so.' She reached for a tissue to wipe peach juice from her chin. 'You know what? Sometimes I think…the way Elliott has reacted…it's all too hard. Maybe I should just drop it.'

It would save Elliott grief. And Sir Frank. Although…would it? Connor met her wistful blue gaze, and felt remorse. Did Elliott Fraser deserve to be spared? Surely every child had the right to know where they came from. And who was to say the old man wouldn't welcome the news of a granddaughter?

Once he got used to the idea.

'And listen,' she said, startling him with her uncanny ability to read his mind, 'I have to ask that you keep this confidential. I've promised Elliott.'

But *he* hadn't.

She gazed anxiously at him. 'You're not thinking of telling his father, are you? That would be shocking for poor Elliott if the old man finds out from someone else. Elliott needs to break the news himself. Please, Connor.' She put her hand on his arm. Her eyes were filled with such urgency, he wavered. 'Elliott might come round, he might see the light and realise it's lovely to have another child in the world. Let him be the one who tells his father.' She leaned forward and the T-shirt slipped and showed him an alluring creamy swell.

'Can't you see? If you tell Sir Frank, Elliott will blame me. He's bound to. And it will be my fault. You'd never have known at all if I hadn't lost that letter.'

Or if he hadn't been so tied up in knots with lust that his brain hadn't been working.

He hesitated. He owed Sir Frank the truth. The investigation had stretched on long enough and he'd used up weeks of his leave already. How much longer would Elliott Fraser stonewall? To Connor's mind, most good-hearted men in Elliott's position would have opened their doors to their lost child by this stage, discreetly, if not with enthusiasm.

But he concealed from her his cynical reading of the man. Sophy Woodruff seemed to have a boundless belief in people who had let her down, and he didn't want to be the one to damage it.

'Sir Frank's an old man,' he pointed out. 'He won't last for ever. If Elliott doesn't tell him, he might miss out on his chance to know you. Now *that* would be a tragedy.'

'No, but… Oh, promise me, Connor. Please.'

She smelled tantalisingly of peach. The pleading in her eyes dragged at something in his chest. With her soft, swollen mouth, the exposure of one smooth shoulder in the absurdly large shirt, she was too desirable for all these worries. What she needed was more kissing to warm her through.

Perhaps she was right, though, and Elliott deserved a chance. She might have a lot to lose if he blew the gaff. On the other hand, there was his commitment. The old guy was relying on him. He *trusted* him.

Either way, someone could get hurt.

He felt a chill misgiving at how it would be for her if Elliott Fraser rejected her.

In the end he compromised. 'Look, I don't feel as if I can promise. I might run into Sir Frank at some time, and then I'd feel awful for concealing something so important from him. But we'll see how it goes with Elliott. If by…say…the autumn…he shows signs of acting like a human being, then we'll see. Here, let me,' he said as she peered down her T-shirt and tried to mop between her breasts with a tissue. 'I can clean this up for you.'

Autumn.

The word sank through Sophy's conscious mind and into a deeper region, where instincts and inspirations combined with clues and intelligence to give her ideas that weren't always welcome. But she pushed this one away from her. Heavens, it was raining, the trees were getting a drink, it was Saturday, and she was in bed with a big, warm, sexy man.

She stayed there for most of Saturday. Connor O'Brien had much to teach her about the erotic arts, he said, and she was a willing pupil. The laundry service returned her clothes in the afternoon, but as it turned out she didn't need them until the next day, when the sky cleared to a joyous blue.

Connor's house wasn't gloomy in daylight. In spite of its neglected feel, it was full of light. The once lush terraced garden was overgrown with wild creepers, and, though there was a private landing stage for the O'Brien boat, no vessel was moored there.

From its location on the Point there were spectacular views in every direction, from the postcard view of the Opera House and the Harbour Bridge, right out to the Manly Heads. She glanced around at all the overgrown shrubs, their leaves plump and juicy with water, and wished she had some secateurs with her.

In the afternoon Connor took her strolling through the Sunday markets at the Rocks, where they gazed at exotic treasures and bought each other souvenirs from a stall that sold stuffed-animal toys. Increasingly conscious of the weekend coming to a close, and her time running out, Sophy secreted her precious koala in the safe zip section of her bag. Soon he would take her home.

On their walk he paused to stare through the window of a bazaar that sold oriental rugs. She tried to read his gaze. She could tell he loved the East by the way he talked about it. Were those foreign scenes calling to him, drawing him back? He surprised her then by striding inside and negotiating with the rug seller for an enormous Kashmiri rug. The man rolled it out on the floor. It was pure silk, in delicate shades of pinks and lavenders, blues and creams, the colours changing from whichever angle they were viewed.

She wished she could take off her shoes, and let her feet sink into its gorgeous pile and wallow.

Watching her with a knowing glint in his eye, Connor said, 'In case you feel like a nap. Let's take it home and try it.'

She was thrilled to the soul. This didn't sound like goodbye, Sophy Woodruff.

When he did take her home to her place, drowsy and languorous with love in the early hours of Monday, he didn't come inside. He kissed her lingeringly at the door, then turned and walked down the path while she watched his retreating back from inside the door, wonder in her heart. How could she, Sophy Woodruff, be desired by a man like Connor O'Brien?

The piles of gear were back in the hall, and she realised with delight that Leah and Zoe were home. Would they believe her fantastic luck? She tiptoed to avoid waking them, only stumbling and barking her shins once, then slipped into bed, hugging her happiness to herself.

Every summer day after that was a precious, golden day. She met Connor before work, on the mornings he didn't drive her there from his place after she'd spent the night. He walked across to the Gardens with her at lunchtime, his lunch, like hers, in a paper bag from the basement deli. Perhaps sensing they'd be intruders, other people stayed away from the willow lawn, and she and Connor had it all to themselves.

Revelling in their privacy, he teased and flirted with her, argued about movies, snatched her novel from her and read steamy excerpts aloud to make her laugh. Sometimes, though, hearing the evocative words in his deep voice would make her hot, and she'd sense from his thickening tones and the spark in his eyes that he was affected, too. Then he'd throw the book aside, grab her and push her down on the grass.

Lying in his arms in the grass, drowning in his kisses, was a dangerous pursuit, because now a kiss was never enough. More than once, passion leaped out of control, and they were forced to hurry back to the Alexandra, running the gamut of the lift and the walk along the gallery, avoiding touching each other while their burning bodies raged to be assuaged. Then she would slip into Connor's office with him for hot, urgent sex. With just enough of each other's clothes removed to make it possible, he would lift her onto his desk and thrust into her, every sizzling stroke a delicious, searing ecstasy, until he raised her to such a wild climax he or she had to cover her mouth to prevent her rapturous cries from exposing their forbidden delight.

At first, in the evenings he took her to restaurants, although increasingly, as the demands of their passion accelerated, it was easier, and more private, to eat at his place and cook for themselves. Connor's kitchen equipment was limited, so it became necessary to go to a kitchen store and buy utensils and a non-stick frying pan with a lid. She went with him, and argued over the merits of the different brands.

In the same week, out of concern for her comfort, Connor bought two rather sumptuous sofas to go with the rug, as well as a deep reclining armchair and a coffee table.

Life had never felt so fantastic. Somehow, the sheer, joyous excitement of being with Connor seemed to spill over and touch everything. The hours she spent with Leah and Zoe, though restricted, seemed more fun than ever, her work with the children more pleasurable.

She was living in an exuberant whirlpool, all anxieties on hold, when she lifted the phone one morning to hear the voice of Elliott Fraser.

Well, well. What had taken him so long?

He regretted the delay, he said in his dry, cool tones. Pressure of work, but he was eager to make good his offer of dinner and a proper discussion.

The night he suggested was her netball night, but she agreed without hesitation and wrote down the address. The Avengers would locate a stand-in for her without much trouble. Instinctively, she decided to keep the invitation to herself. It was a private contract between her and her father, and, depending on the success of it, she'd report back to Connor. She acknowledged something to herself then that she'd sensed in her heart. Though he'd never stated it, Connor didn't have a very high opinion of Elliott. If things didn't turn out well, she'd hate him to think she looked like a needy little loser.

Better to see how things went.

Since the address Elliott gave her was a fair distance from home, she chose to drive. She took along a bottle of wine, out of courtesy, although she wouldn't be indulging herself.

She felt mildly surprised by 221 Enfield Place. It was a modest brick and tile home with a small garden behind a high hedge. When she rang the doorbell, a woman in an overall with a pleasant face opened the door and invited her in, introducing herself as Marie, and explaining that Mr Fraser had been delayed. She showed Sophy down a short hall into a sitting room with an adjoining dining room. Marie took the wine from her and offered her a glass, but Sophy declined, accepting the offer of soft drink instead.

Savoury food smells suggested that dinner was well under way.

Marie brought her lemonade, then returned to her cooking, while Sophy sat on a stiff sofa with cylindrical steel legs and inspected the room. The carpet had an all-over autumnal pattern. The autumn theme was continued in the pictures on the walls, some lake and forest scenes in over-vivid shades that suggested mass production.

A cabinet stood against one wall, with a small lamp and a couple of photos in frames. One was of a much younger Elliott Fraser, the other was a magnificently gilded one of his wedding party, and looked as if it would be more appropriately placed in Buckingham Palace than this unpretentious suburban room.

Sophy got up and walked over for a closer look. The wedding

looked like the high-society occasion she might have expected, with the bride and bridesmaids in couture gowns.

The room held no sign of a child. Where was he? she wondered, turning to investigate the dining room. The table was set for two. Perhaps Matthew was being minded by someone, although…

Something about the place gave her a prickly sensation of discomfort. The furnishings were adequate, but somehow sterile like those in the first room. Not really what she'd have expected of the residence of the wealthy man Connor had described.

A depressed feeling descended upon her. All at once she knew with certainty Elliott didn't live here.

Following the aromas, she walked through to the kitchen. Marie had dinner plates on the warming hob, and was mixing some sort of sauce. She looked up in surprise.

'Sorry for intruding,' Sophy said with a smile. 'I just wondered something, Marie. Mind if I ask? Have you been cooking for Mr Fraser long?'

The woman paused her stirring. 'No, well, love, I don't stay on. I'm a temp, really. This is my first job for Mr Fraser. I think it's just for the one night, although he said there was a slight chance there might have to be more coming up.'

'Did he?' Sophy smiled, though she could feel the weight on her heart like a stone. More coming up. In case she wasn't convinced the first time. For a while her head swam in disbelief while she tried to process it.

Why had he attempted such a cheap, despicable trick? For fear she would contaminate his real home? Or…an even more contemptible possibility occurred to her. Was it a ploy to conceal his massive wealth from her, in case she got ideas? She felt enveloped in a choking shame. Where was his integrity? How could she be related to a man with so little honour?

'Look, Marie, the dinner smells lovely, but I'm sorry I won't be able to stay. Will you please tell Mr Fraser I'm not hungry?'

She let herself out the front door, and as she stepped off the small patio started when her attention was drawn by a man getting out of a dark, sleek car parked in the driveway. It was Elliott, looking grim-faced, his movements hurried and rather jerky as he stooped and reached into the backseat for something.

As he straightened he saw her and jolted upright, then closed the car door and strode along the cement path that crossed the lawn, smoothing back his silver hair. 'Miss Woo— Sophy.' He extended a hand, then his eyes focused on her face and he dropped the attempt. 'What're you…? You're not leaving?'

'I am, yes, but you don't have to worry, Mr Fraser. I won't cause you any trouble. You have nothing to fear from me.' She felt her throat swell, but held back the tears. 'I won't bother you again.'

He stood there looking thunderstruck as she turned to walk down the path, then he hastened to catch her at the gate. 'Miss Woodruff… Sophy…what's this about? Has something happened? What has my housekeeper been—'

She paused outside the gate and turned. 'Don't, please. Don't make it worse. I'd rather remember you as someone with dignity, at least.'

His face contorted and anger flashed in his chill grey eyes. 'Look, how have you missed out, just answer me that? You had good parents, from all accounts. A good family life. How could I have raised you on my own? After your mother died, it was the best option. You come after me, wanting answers, harassing me. Just *who* do you think—'

'Who do I think I am?' She faced him proudly, the barest tremble in her low, cool voice. 'I'm Sophy Woodruff. That's who. And whoever *you* are is nothing to do with me.'

All at once she felt sorry for Elliott Fraser. Without looking at him again she got into the car, started it at once and drove away. Away from his pathetic subterfuge, his decoy home and the flimsy hedge he'd erected against the monstrous threat she posed.

After a long while she realised she was shaking and travelling in the wrong direction. She had to turn back and drive around for ages, in and out of unfamiliar streets, before she could find any landmarks she recognised. At last, by accident, she stumbled back onto the road to Bondi Junction. She headed up the hill, through Woollahra, and joined the artery that would take her to Point Piper.

CHAPTER TWELVE

CONNOR O'Brien wasn't expecting her, that much was clear. When he opened the door he stood there with such a veiled, stern expression, Sophy's heart plunged, realising she'd never just dropped by before, and wondered if she'd crossed some invisible line. Then his lean face relaxed and he smiled. 'Ah. Come in.'

Too late, though. That first impression sank in like indelible ink. 'What's the matter, Connor?' she said in an attempt to smile it away. 'You haven't got a blonde in here, have you?'

'The blonde's just left. Now I'm ready for a brunette.' He spoke lightly, but his eyes were hooded. He gestured her in and she started down the hall ahead of him. They reached the sitting room and he stood with his hands tucked into the pockets of his jeans. There was an awkward moment, then he said, 'Is anything wrong?'

He looked more closely at her, then reached out to touch her, but she backed away, suddenly seeing how it would be if she broke down and sobbed on his shoulder like a whining wimp.

Without properly meeting his eyes, she gave a shrug. 'Just thought I'd drop by. See if you had plans. In case you felt like some gorgeous feminine company.' She smiled and fluttered her lashes at him, slipped off her shoulder bag. Her glance fell on his laptop, open on the coffee table.

He followed her gaze and made a swift, smooth movement to close it.

She remembered then that Connor had a life she wasn't privy to. An unpleasant realisation dawned on her. Being his lover didn't automatically give her rights. She shouldn't have assumed she could just drop in, and expect him to…what? Drop everything? Comfort her while she bled all over him like a needy child? More than ever this visit felt like a transgression. After all the fun and excitement of their daily contacts, she couldn't help feeling hurt, and a warning sense of panic. Heavens, what with having unrealistic expectations of Elliott, and now Connor, she had to wonder if she could ever trust herself to get anything right.

She could see him studying her, his black brows drawn, a question in his intelligent dark eyes, and she tried to conceal the black, leaden weight on her heart.

'Oh, look, Connor. I see you're working. Sorry. I shouldn't have interrupted you without warning. Very insensitive of me.' She took up her bag again, slung it on her shoulder and flashed him an unfocused grin. 'I'll take myself off.'

Recognising too late that his responses had been inadequate, Connor put out a hand to halt her. 'Hang on.' Her arm felt quite cold. In the stronger light he could see he hadn't imagined her pallor, the brittleness behind her smile. 'Isn't this your netball night?'

'Yes, well, usually. I…er…couldn't go tonight.'

He frowned. 'But—you always go. You love the Avengers.'

'I know.' She hesitated a second, her face working with the effort to conceal some inexpressible emotion, then she turned towards the hall, giving him a backwards wave. 'Anyway, I'd better go. See you.'

A quick succession of thoughts and feelings flashed through him. Consternation, remorse. Something was wrong, she'd chosen to tell him, but he'd been too concerned at being dragged away from his communication with the embassy, and failed the test.

He had to stride to catch up with her at the door. 'What's wrong?' She stood with her back to him, her hand on the knob, and he saw her brace her slim shoulders against some heavy weight. 'Sweetheart, what is it? What's happened?' Then he guessed. 'Oh, no. Don't tell me. You've been to see Elliott Fraser.'

She didn't answer. He gripped her upper arms and he could feel the tremor in them. He turned her to face him. She gave a twisted attempt at a smile that wrenched his heart.

'Connor…' She breathed in with difficulty. 'Would you mind just putting your arms around me for a second?'

'Sophy, Sophy…' He held her as close as it was feasible without crushing her, stroking her hair, wishing he could go to Elliott Fraser's house and confront the man with his cold, patrician face. Little by little he prised it out of her, the phony house, the confrontation at the gate.

He tried to limit himself to murmuring soothing things in her ear, but the fragrance of her hair and her supple, vibrant body had their inevitable effect, and before he knew it he was kissing away her tears, then kissing her for real.

The next thing he knew he was as hard as granite, stripping off her clothes with shaky hands, his heart thundering in his ears as he laid her on his bed and felt the passion rise to consume them.

As always, she offered herself to him with such ardent, unfettered trust he felt awed. Uncritical of his rough, masculine solution to every agony of the spirit, she returned his caresses with as much fervour as before. Her responsiveness as he tasted the treasures of her body were even more passionate.

It wasn't just his imagination. The playful eroticism of their previous couplings was swamped by a powerful emotional current that connected her to him at some deep level. The intensity moved him so deeply he felt shaken. In some way, the primitive core of him opened up to the harmony of two souls mingling, like a dry desert gulch welcoming rain.

His brain tried to warn him of the deadly danger of what had happened, what he was doing, but he was beyond reason.

As he positioned himself to take her, gazing down at her delicately flushed face, his lust was infused with the most overwhelming tenderness. Concepts like rules and responsibility were meaningless when faced with his poignant urgency to drive the shadows from Sophy Woodruff's eyes.

He plunged into her, groaning with the almost unbearable pleasure of sliding into her moist heat.

Then he rocked her, tenderly stroking the smooth satin walls yielding before him with such a delicious friction, all the time holding her fervent gaze. Unable to restrain his sinuous movements for long, he thrust faster and faster, deeper, harder, while she dug her nails into his back, her face and neck strained with the sweet tension.

With every stroke he felt himself wanting to bind her closer, his thundering heart awash with emotions he'd forgotten he could feel, passion and possession, and an aching need to somehow protect her from all the tragedies of existence.

With a massive effort of will he held back his own rising pleasure to keep pace with hers, until he was nearly ready to explode.

At last, he felt the convulsive tightening grip of her muscles, saw her eyes close, the wave of ecstasy ripple over her face, and allowed himself to soar to his own crescendo and let his searing-hot seed spurt in a fantastic, rapturous release.

Afterwards, though, while she slept snuggled into the curve of his body, Connor lay wide-awake and stared into the grim dark.

His body felt energised, fulfilled and at ease, while a hopeless dismay invaded his soul.

What had he done? The very thing, the *one* thing he knew he must not. He'd let emotion in, and lost his sense of perspective.

What a self-indulgent fool. He could see how, little by little, he'd succumbed. He'd turned every incident to his advantage to have her, a tender woman, a *virgin*, for God's sake. He'd played with her, seduced her, romanced her, and now…

His gut churned with the awful guilt.

Now she depended on him.

No use to remind himself she wasn't a child, she was responsible for her own actions, her own risks. At that first peal of the doorbell earlier that evening he'd recognised the damage he'd done.

He'd forgotten his code. Forgotten that people in ordinary walks of life needed the invisible tendrils of relationship to connect them, keep them safe and supported. Allowed himself to link with her. Encouraged her to trust him.

And who would she have when he was gone?

CHAPTER THIRTEEN

'OH, IT'S just so *mean* keeping such a beautiful animal in prison. Look into those eyes, Connor. Don't you wish you could set him free?'

Sophy glanced up at him but he wasn't looking at her. He was staring through the glass at the leopard, but with such grimness in his fathomless dark gaze she realised with a small tremor of fear that he was looking beyond the magnificent creature, at something remote and internal.

'What, Connor? What is it?'

She didn't expect an answer. Not a true one. And she didn't want one. Since the night she'd dropped in on him, Connor had changed. She blamed herself, of course. She'd done the thing Leah and Zoe had often shaken their heads over in regard to other poor, foolhardy women.

She'd exposed her true feelings. Not in what she'd actually said, but in so many other ways. And now he'd retreated to some distant region, and she felt helpless to change things back to the way they had been. She supposed she could try to pretend not to feel anything, but there was no fooling him. She read his comprehension of her weakness in every dark glance. It made her painfully unable to be natural with him.

Every time she opened her mouth, she could feel him tense, as if she might be about to blurt out the fateful word. And she could hardly trust herself not to. So often now, especially when they were making love, she longed to tell him, to somehow ease her soul of its aching burden. But it didn't take Einstein to know what would happen if she did, and how that gaping black universe might feel.

'Sorry? Come this way,' he said. 'Let's see what's down here.'

They strolled away from the big cats, and headed down a wide avenue where the sound of trumpeting and heavy shuffling were drawing a crowd. She'd brought a shady hat with her, for though the leaves were on the turn, the sun was still strong. She put it on now, grateful for the wide brim's usefulness in concealing her face when she needed to.

Her lover looked so lean, tanned and handsome in his jeans and a snowy white polo shirt, if it hadn't been for the tension in him she'd have felt proud. Every so often he took her hand and held it for short bursts, and she saw other women look at her with envy. If only they knew how tenuous her happiness was.

She felt so sorry for the poor elephant, rocking backwards and forwards like an unloved child, a heavy chain on its leg. She glanced at Connor to see what he made of it, but his attention was suddenly turned on some people approaching down the path from the other direction. He was watching the approach of an elderly gent with a stick, who was doing his best to keep up with a very small boy in a Spiderman costume. A man in a chauffeur's uniform followed them at a respectful distance.

As they drew near the old man spotted Connor, and his face lit up in recognition. 'Well, well, now. Connor O'Brien.' He halted and leaned on his stick. 'Now, isn't this a splendid coincidence? Good to see you, my boy.' His bright eyes darted straight to Sophy.

Connor stepped forward to shake hands, enquiring warmly about the old gent's health. The boy's gaze was fixed on the commotion surrounding the elephant, then he turned Sophy's way. With a severe shock she recognised the intense, eager little face of Matthew Fraser.

'Come and say hello to Mr O'Brien, Matthew,' the old man commanded.

With her head still spinning, she hardly heard Connor's murmured greeting to the child, and when he drew her forward and said, 'Sir Frank, this is Sophy Woodruff. Sir Frank Fraser, Sophy,' the words were so momentous, they took a while to connect.

So this was her grandfather. The old man nodded his head at her, and held out his wrinkled hand. He smelled of mints and eucalyptus. 'Well, well. So you're Sophy Woodruff.' He peered at her with curiosity. 'Do you like the zoo, Sophy?'

'I...I like the animals,' she hedged, not wanting to disappoint him. She glanced at Connor, but he'd slipped on his sunglasses and his eyes were inaccessible.

Sir Frank turned his attention back to him, though he kept glancing at her as he made elderly small talk. Connor's responses were smooth and respectful. She could sense that, despite the careful conversation, he and the old man were very familiar with each other. And she knew something else with absolute certainty.

This was a set-up.

She'd thought it strange when Connor had suggested an afternoon at the zoo. But how much had he told the old man? Was he aware she was his granddaughter?

Oblivious of the concerns of the adults, Matthew grew bored with the conversation and commandeered a park bench under a nearby tree for a game of climbing up one end, running along and jumping off, until his grandfather called him over.

'Sit down here with me awhile, my dear,' Sir Frank said, patting Sophy's hand. 'Here, young fella. Take Connor for a walk and show him that elephant.'

She allowed Sir Frank to usher her to the bench and commence a gentle, probing inquisition about her job, her interests and her friends. He was a charmer. Normally she'd have been enchanted, but there were so many vibrations and dangerous cross-currents on the air that, though she answered everything politely, she couldn't keep her attention from Connor and the boy.

True to his grandfather's instructions, the child took a couple of brave steps towards Connor, who stood in silence, his hands hooked into his jeans. He made no gesture of encouragement. She saw Matthew gaze up at his intimidating height, and wait for some sign from behind the dark glasses. The little boy's feet faltered.

He cast an anxious glance over his shoulder at his grandfather.

Sophy tensed and sat very still, her breath on hold as Connor surveyed the child in a sort of frozen immobility. At last he appeared to thaw. He relaxed his posture and held out his hand. 'All right, Spiderman,' he said, a smile in his deep voice. 'Show me an elephant.'

She heaved a secret sigh of relief, and became aware of Sir Frank studying her with a shrewd gaze. 'No need to worry about Connor. He'd never hurt a little one. He had a son of his own, you know. Things go wrong in families, my dear, as you'd know in your line of work.'

The old man rambled on, about fathers and sons and mothers and daughters, but all the time she couldn't take her eyes off Connor and the child. Watching him looking down at Matthew, listening to his chatter, strolling along and holding his hand, pointing things out to him, lifting him up to see over the heads of the crowd. She was overwhelmed then with the saddest, most poignant feeling of regret she could ever remember, a feeling so painful and intense she knew her heart would break.

Connor O'Brien was the perfect man for her. And she could see it all clearly now. She knew why he couldn't meet her eyes. Why he was introducing her to these strangers.

He was leaving her.

The journey to Point Piper seemed very long. She made a few listless enquiries.

'Does Sir Frank know everything?' she asked.

He glanced at her, then his eyes slid away. 'Look—I felt I had to tell him. It seemed—necessary. You don't really mind, do you?' She gave a shrug and he made an attempt at encouragement. 'You know, he's not at all the same person as Elliott. He's quite a—a grand old guy. My own father thought the world of him. And you're like him in some ways. Amazingly.'

'Really?'

He must have heard the lack of enthusiasm in her voice, because his brows lifted. 'I'm surprised. I thought this meant so much to you, getting to know your birth family.'

They'd turned down a street lined with plane trees. She noticed they had a sad, yellowy, autumn look. 'Yes, well, it's not as simple as I thought. Nothing ever is, is it?'

She felt his swift glance on her face.

'Are you hurt that I told him?'

She tried to smile. 'How could I be? I know why you did it.'

His jaw tightened and he was silent for a second. 'Look—look, sweetheart, it doesn't have to change anything if you don't want it to, does it? There's nothing to say you *have* to have him in your life.'

'Sounds as if you're sweet-talking me, Connor. But there's no need.' She gave a weary sigh. 'Let's face it. There's no saying I'll ever hear from him again. He's met me now and satisfied his curiosity. What more is there to expect, really?'

And to be honest, right then she didn't even want to think about the Frasers. All her hopes in that direction seemed like the naive, girlish dream of the person she used to be. Before she found what she really wanted. Before she grew up.

They lapsed into silence after that.

When they arrived at Connor's, he quickly disappeared to the kitchen to make coffee, then brought the cups in and set them on the coffee table. Props for the death scene. She wished she weren't so good at picking up vibrations.

Here it was. The kiss-off.

And so soon, she kept thinking. She'd known all along it was coming, but somehow she still wasn't prepared.

Connor invited her to sit. When had they become so formal with each other? He took the adjoining sofa, leaning forward and frowning down at his clasped hands. The world seemed to slow down, or perhaps it was her heart.

Luckily for her, adrenaline kicked in.

'Sophy. There's something I need to talk about…' He closed his eyes for an instant. 'To *tell* you…'

She raised her eyes to his. 'I know what you're going to say.' Her voice sounded as raspy as if she'd been living on dry biscuits for a year.

His gaze sharpened. 'You know. *What* do you know?'

'You're going away.'

'*How* do you…?' He closed his eyes again, as if meeting hers was too difficult. 'All right. It's true. I have a job on the other side of the world. And I have to go. It's as simple as that. This…this is what I do.'

It was her old dilemma. Whether to fight, to plead, cajole and manipulate to hold the people she loved, or to accept the verdict with dignity and let them go. Either way, they left in the end.

She tried to keep her voice firm. 'I thought you said your contract had finished.'

'Yes. I…did say that. It had finished. But I—I've been given the option to renew it.'

'I see.'

That was painful, but there was worse to come.

Connor's lean hands curled into fists. She could see the sinews ridging along the insides of his wrists. 'No, I don't think you—you really understand. I'm— This isn't easy for me. It's not easy for me to just—leave. To—leave you.'

She smiled at him, though it scraped the sore spot in her chest. 'Well, you could always stay. Save yourself some heartache.'

A muscle tightened in his cheek. Then he leaned forward and took her trembling hands, his dark eyes grave. 'My position as a lawyer is just one of the jobs I do at the embassy. There's another one I'm committed to, as well. I have to return to fulfil that.'

'What do you mean? What is it?'

'It's—intelligence. I collect information.'

She sat up straight and widened her eyes. 'What? Do you mean—like a spy?'

He flushed a little. 'Not exactly. Not like something you see in the movies. But I do—have to—keep contact with a—a network of people. Sometimes I have to meet people in quite dangerous locations.'

Ridiculous lurid scenes from James Bond, sadistic villains, dark alleys and spectacular car crashes flitted through her mind. 'Well, do you shadow people? Bug their phones?'

He was silent for a couple of heartbeats, then said, 'I can't really talk about this. It's serious business. National security. People's lives are at stake.'

Her life was at stake, but she didn't like to mention it, although she felt a sudden numbing roar in her ears. 'So—let me get this straight. This time you've been here now—were you ever really planning to stay?'

His eyes slid away from hers. 'Not really. I came out here for a break.' He shook his head and held up his hand as if to forestall her reaction. 'No, there's no need to say it. I know. I should never—never have… I had no right to get involved with you.'

'So all the time you've been here—you've been on *holiday*?'

He gave a cautious nod.

'But you took the rooms at the Alexandra. Well, then… I mean—have you been doing intelligence work here?'

He lowered his eyes and made a sharp intake of breath. 'Look…Sophy…'

A horrible possibility began to emerge from the mists, almost laughable at first, until it began to take shape.

'You know, it's a funny thing…' her voice sounded as husky as a soul sister's in a film noir classic '…but when I first knew you, I often had this really strong feeling that you were right there, close by, wherever I went. As if you were *following* me. I kept telling myself I was imagining things.' She gazed at him long and hard. 'Were you, Connor? Were you—what do you call it?—keeping me under surveillance?'

He flinched a little, but his dark eyes met hers with grim honesty. 'For a while.'

'Oh.' The pain was so extreme. As the blood drained from her heart the world as she'd known it for the past few months kaleidoscoped and reassembled itself into a new agonising pattern.

All the romance, the laughter and excitement, the passion. What had it been, really?

The answer sliced through her. A sham.

She closed her eyes, and the next word escaped as a croak. 'Why?'

He continued to meet her eyes with his grim, bleak gaze. 'As a favour to someone. Someone who mistakenly felt his family was under threat.'

She stared at him as the full, indigestible truth finally began to penetrate her numb brain. His rooms at the Alexandra. Getting to know her. Bringing her home with him. Making love to her. Securing her trust, her confidence.

Her eternal, undying love.

'Oh. Oh, I see.' Her eyes filled with tears, and through the mist she noticed the faintest sheen on his handsome forehead, but she had shock and betrayal to contend with, and didn't have room for pity.

She held her fists to her chest. 'I feel like such a fool. It was Elliott, I suppose. You were doing a favour for him. Keeping me occupied and away from him.' Her lips were nearly too dry to move. 'Goodness. He must be a really important man.'

'No, no, *not* Elliott,' he corrected swiftly, almost as if that would have been an insult. 'Look, I shouldn't be telling you this, but I'm trying to be honest with you. I owe you that much.' She flashed him a wry look and the stain across his cheekbones deepened. 'It—it was Sir Frank. He was worried—he wanted me to find out why you were meeting his son.' He made a jerky movement with his hands and said, 'And I was not *keeping you occupied*. You must know it's *not*—it never has been like that. I was with you for the same reason any guy would want to be with you.' His face was so stiff and controlled, she had to wonder what emotions were contained behind the rock face. Call her gullible, but she actually believed what he was saying.

'But—' his lean hands lifted '—I really can't stay. I tried to tell you that once before. I'm—not the man for you.'

She twisted her hands in her lap. 'I know. I remember... But that was before we...'

Fell in love.

'But, Connor, *maybe...*'

Maybe she was wrong. Maybe no part of his heart had ever been involved. She loved him so much she'd imagined it was reciprocated, when what she was really seeing and feeling was a mere reflection. Everyone knew secret agents were good at divorcing their emotions from their work. Look at James Bond. A different woman in every city.

With her pride, her life hanging in the balance, she hardly dared frame the words. 'Maybe there are children over there who need a speech-language pathologist.'

He sat very still, his lashes lowered while his sharp brain registered her brazen proposal. What else was it, after all? Whoever heard of a diplomat turning up with a speech-language pathologist? He'd have to marry her.

Her hopes, her most secret dreams, her foolish love-struck heart all waited, quivering, beneath the guillotine.

'Sophy.' His eyes were cool and steady, and she could see he'd switched off his emotions to deal with her in secret-agent mode. 'It's the most dangerous place on earth. The work I do there— Try to understand. My wife, my *son* died flying out there to meet me. I— I really can't be responsible for another human being.'

She flushed at that. 'I'm responsible for myself, Connor.'

She didn't stay long then. She wasn't the woman to use her wiles to trap a man, even if she'd had any. Deceit wasn't in her repertoire.

To her mind it all came down to love, and the elusive nature of it. In her experience, there was no way of forcing someone to love you.

Connor didn't want her to drive him to the airport. Perhaps she should have been relieved, but that seemed as cruel as the rest of it. However hurtful it felt to see her lover leave, it was the *seeing* that mattered. Every tiny last fraction of a second of *seeing* him was precious, to be treasured and stored in a vaccuum-sealed part of her heart until she was too old to care or remember. He just mustn't have felt the same way about her.

After that final goodbye, not many mornings passed before she ran up the stairs in the Alexandra to see that his name had been re-moved from his door. His books and certificates were gone. Every trace he'd ever been there, ever teased her, laughed with her, kissed her under the willow tree…gone.

She'd expected it daily. But it was a blow.

The Alexandra was a desolate place.

There were some things a woman didn't feel like confiding, even to her best friends. By the way Zoe and Leah tiptoed around her at home, though, it seemed likely they guessed. Even the staff at work seemed to treat her with kid gloves. But people had to move on, even when they were broken and dying inside, and she still had children depending on her and a life to haul back onto the tracks. It was a lesson she'd learned before. To be happy again, she had to *be* happy. She needed to be positive and upbeat, and show the world she was fine.

Which was why, when she received an elegantly embossed invi-tation in the mail to attend Sir Frank Fraser's ninetieth birthday cele-bration, she sat down after a few moments, and wrote an acceptance.

CHAPTER FOURTEEN

WHAT was the perfect gift for a nonagenarian with a sharp, lively mind? In what Sophy hoped was an inspiration, she decided on a small volume of wry, clever verse from an Australian poet of the same extraordinary vintage as Sir Frank, and wrapped it in silver paper.

She started dressing early. For luck, as much as the exclusive Vaucluse address, she'd bought a new dress for the occasion. Its silvery blue chiffon clung to her curves. There was a faint shimmer in the fabric when she moved that seemed to lend a pale luminosity to her skin.

She'd had her hair straightened, and it hung below her shoulders, as glossy and silken as a shampoo model's. She just hoped she hadn't gone overboard.

All day long she'd experienced warning prickles up and down her spine, as if something portentous was about to happen, and sure enough, late in the afternoon, at the exact moment when she was thinking of phoning for a taxi, a man called to inform her that a limousine was on its way to collect her.

Heavens. She felt overwhelmed by such unexpected consideration. In truth, the surprise nearly brought on an anxiety attack. The old gent certainly knew how to roll out the red.

The limo arrived on time. She recognised Sir Frank's driver, and as he transported her through the gathering dusk, felt her nervousness subside into a taut anticipation.

Set behind high iron gates, Sir Frank's home was an imposing stone mansion. When she arrived, the party appeared to be already under way, with people spilling from the front entrance. As she alighted from the car more guests were being set down.

She was greeted by a middle-aged woman who directed her through the noisy crowd in the large, elegant vestibule to the morning room.

She threaded her way through and found her host surrounded by well-wishers, among a mass of presents and wrapping paper. When he caught sight of her, he broke into an elderly beam, and exclaimed, 'Ah, Sophy, Sophy. Here you are.'

She presented her small offering, and brushed cheeks with him. Then he turned excitedly to the people on either side of him. 'Now, this is Sophy Woodruff. Sit here beside me, Sophy. Hey, you there, matey, this young woman needs a drink.'

A white-coated boy bearing a tray sprang to instant obedience and brought her a glass of champagne. She found herself warmly greeted on all sides, though, of course, Sir Frank's friends and relations wouldn't have known who she was to the family. Elliott hadn't arrived yet, Sir Frank told her in a low voice. Something about his wife having returned from overseas.

She was relieved about that. The occasion was fraught enough for her as it was. In fact, it was really very emotional. Despite the evident wealth of his home, the fleet of waiters and caterers, she found a homely kindness in the old man's welcome that was so moving, a lump rose in her throat.

After a full-on thirty minutes of chatter and friendly enquiries she had to excuse herself for a brief spell, for fear of disgracing herself with tears. But, of course, these days she was an emotional *Titanic*.

She wandered outside, where tables and chairs were set on a terrace beside the pool.

Lights glimmered on the harbour, their glow intensifying in the deepening twilight. Below the balustrade of the terrace, a lush, softly lit garden flowed down to the water's edge. Steps built into the hillside led down to a picturesque, old-fashioned jetty where some of the guests had moored their boats.

This was how Connor's garden could look, she reflected, if anyone had been there to tend it.

A sleek motor launch, lights ablaze, nudged alongside the jetty. More wealthy people, she guessed, come to pay their respects.

It was wonderful, and so unexpected, to be one of the honoured guests, welcomed into the home of a bona fide grandparent. A few months ago nothing could have made her happier. And she *was* happy. She truly was. She had everything to be happy about. A wonderful job she loved, friends, and now a grandfather.

Her eyes grew misty and the cruiser's lights blurred. Face it. The trouble was, no matter how positive and upbeat she pretended to be, she couldn't move on from the terrible black chasm in her soul. In fact, celebrations only made her feel miserable.

Other people made her miserable.

Sunshine and birdsong made her miserable.

When she'd made a discreet dab at her eyes she saw that the man stepping up onto the jetty from the cruiser was really quite tall. From this distance, as indistinct as he was in the dusk, he looked a bit like Connor.

Another cruel twinge. When would she stop imagining him everywhere, dreaming of him, yearning for him? When would she ever get over this aching emptiness?

She strained to watch the new arrival, noting his long, easy stride as he headed for the steps and disappeared from her view.

The trouble was, the things that had eased her spirit in the past were unavailable to her now. She couldn't go to the Gardens. She had to avoid all parks and green places for fear of sighting a willow. Even the moon could make her cry. And there it was again, slyly swimming up over the headland, mocking her with its pale glory.

The man's dark head came into view as he climbed the steps.

She tensed, and her heart beat painfully fast. He looked so like *him*.

He lifted his head, and she felt certain he was looking straight at her. He *was* Connor. He had to be. Unless she was hallucinating again. She remembered then that actually she never *had* been hallucinating. He had been there all the time, shadowing her like a ghost. As the man drew nearer he quickened his stride, then broke into a run.

Her own personal ghost materialised from the indigo dusk, but at the very last his steps faltered. 'Sophy?'

He must have noticed her shocked, incredulous face, because with a little groan he surged forward, threw his arms around her and crushed her to his big, hard body.

'Oh, Sophy, my darling, my darling.'

It was Connor O'Brien, it really was him in the flesh. *His* hands, *his* lips, and his big strong heart beating against hers and making her burst into tears.

He kissed her wet face, and smoothed her hair, caressing her all over as if his hands had to reassure themselves of the feel of her, while her starved body hugged him to her, breathed in the familiar scent of him.

Eventually he stopped kissing her and held her away from him, while she issued a stream of barely coherent questions.

'Where did you come from? I mean, how long have you…? When did you get the boat? Why…why are you…? Connor? I thought you—had to… I'm in shock.'

'I'm so sorry.' All at once his dark eyes were uncertain, and he dropped his hands. 'I shouldn't have just assumed… I should have let you know. I should have given you time…' He ran a hand through his hair. 'Oh, oh, yes, the boat. I borrowed it from a neighbour. Quickest way here. Are you— Sophy, are you still…? You do seem quite pleased to see me.'

He glanced around then, as though noticing the surroundings for the first time. The crowd had started to trickle onto the terrace. People were noisily chatting, laughing, sipping their drinks, being served food by the platoon of waiters. It was hardly the place for a private reconciliation.

Connor slipped his arm around her. 'My darling, is there anywhere here we can talk?'

With the universe suddenly upside down in a state of joyous confusion, Sophy hardly knew what she said, or if any of it made sense. *My darling* was sounding very positive, though. 'I don't know. It's terribly crowded. Maybe the garden, or inside…'

At that moment Sir Frank, supported by Parkins, emerged from the house, and stood searching the terrace with his bright gaze until he spotted Sophy. 'Ah, there she is.' When he saw Connor, his wispy old eyebrows shot up as far as they could go. 'Connor. *You're* here.'

He shook Parkins off and limped over to them, making amazing progress on his stick, and exchanged an affectionate embrace with Connor. 'I thought you were on the other side of the world.'

Connor smiled and sent her an intense, heart-stopping glance. 'I needed to come back.'

'I knew you would,' the old man exclaimed. 'I had a very strong feeling. Didn't I, Parkins? Isn't that what we said? It's just what we expected. I told you, Parkins, didn't I?'

Not waiting for Parkins's endorsement, he beamed from one to the other of them with such obvious satisfaction, Sophy felt herself blush. It was clear he believed himself involved in a little matchmaking. Little did he know the raw undercurrents that connected her and Connor, for all that first spontaneous burst of joy they'd both expressed in seeing each other.

'Look, Sir Frank,' Connor said, taking swift charge. 'Sorry to rush off from your celebration, but we can't stay. I'm just off a plane, I'm jet-lagged, and I need to sort something out with Sophy. That's if…' He turned to her, his dark eyes soft and intent on hers. 'Will you—will you come home?'

Her heart skipped in her chest, and she nodded with a tremulous hope.

They took their leave, promising to come again, then Connor ushered Sophy down the steps, and along the jetty. She didn't feel dressed for a boat, what with her new chiffon and lucky high heels, but since that first moment of knowing it really was Connor bounding up the steps to her, her excitement had taken such a hold, she was prepared to rough it.

Once on the boat, though, she saw she needn't have worried. People from Point Piper didn't rough things. Connor settled her beside him in a seat that was as sheltered and padded as his big recliner, and wrapped a blanket around her knees. Behind them was a luxurious state room, with deep, inviting sofas cunningly fitted into the walls.

Once he was sure she was comfortable, he started the engine and steered them out into the bay. He seemed to know what he was doing. She felt the most exquisite, bittersweet longing as she gazed at his beautiful, lean hands, so sure and firm on the helm, and her eyes threatened to mist up again.

How she loved those hands.

Even with the moon in the ascendent, the lights around the Sydney shoreline had never glittered more brightly than on this magic night.

Once they were across Rose Bay and had rounded the Point, he cut the engine and she heard the rattle of the anchor chain seeking the murky depths.

In the sudden silence, broken only by the lap of the waves and the distant hoot of a ferry chugging back to the Quay, the cockpit felt as cosy and intimate as a fireside. She had the most thrilling, prickling sensation in the back of her neck.

Something wonderful was about to happen.

'Sophy…' He turned to her, then hesitated, frowning a little as though searching for the right words. 'My darling…'

Lucky for him he had a speech-language pathologist aboard. To help him get started, she said, 'Are you thinking of throwing me overboard? I can swim, you know.'

'I don't doubt it.' He smiled, but his eyes quickly grew serious. 'Sweetheart, I've been such a fool. I'm truly sorry. I know I've cost you—some pain.' He winced.

She lowered her gaze. There was no denying it. After all, she'd given him her all and he'd trashed it.

'I have to tell you something. I've been doing a lot of thinking. I don't want to stay in the Foreign Service.'

She stayed motionless, then said carefully, 'I thought you loved your job there.'

'I did, yes, but I've done it for long enough now. The other part— you know, the intelligence work—I don't want to do anymore. I've been missing out on too much, so I've packed it all in. Both jobs. Cancelled my contract. Left the Service. *Both* services. What do you think?' He looked seriously at her.

'What do *I* think?' Her heart was singing, but she wasn't sure she was entitled to an opinion. 'Well, I think you have to follow your heart.'

He smiled and gave her hands a squeeze. 'You know, until I met you— For years now I've been fooling myself… I *believed* that I could live without—people in my life.' The raw emotion she heard in his voice moved her unbearably. 'It was after the accident I took on the other work. In the end I stayed much longer than I'd ever intended. I guess there seemed no point coming home.' He gave her a rueful glance. 'In order to carry out that work I found I had to live more or less like a machine, with no personal attachments.' He shook his head. '*Crazy*. Thank God at least I managed to see my father before he died. So, when I was sent home on leave and Sir Frank asked me to check out your background—he did me the greatest favour of my life.' His grip on her hands tightened. 'I know it hurt you, but…I'm so grateful. You know, Sophy, from the first minute I saw you…'

'Oh, Connor,' she breathed. 'And from the first moment I saw *you*.'

He kissed her. 'What you saw was a very cynical man. A lost cause. And what *I* saw—' his voice softened '—was a beautiful, innocent girl.'

'Oh, *what*?' She rocked back in her seat. '*Innocent*? I beg your pardon, are you trying to insult me? Where do you think I've been living all my life? In a convent? You'd better realise that just because I happened to be a virgin when we met, it was nothing special. It was a perfectly normal state for me to be in, until I was ready to change it. Being a *virgin* does not have some mythical, magical *stuff* attached to it.' She grinned at him. 'Get with the real world, fella.'

He laughed and kissed her lips, and she felt the fire dance along them with the old rousing charge to her bloodstream.

'No, no, of course it doesn't,' he said smoothly. 'I know that, of course I do. It's just that…well, after I seduced you…'

Sophy gazed at him wide-eyed for a second, then couldn't restrain a laugh. It was quite a low, throaty laugh, probably because she hadn't laughed very often lately.

'So…what makes you think *you* seduced *me*?'

He blinked, then he smiled and his lashes flickered down. 'We-e-ll. All right, then. Perhaps we seduced each other. But what I wanted to say was…if you're ready to hear this…'

'All right. Please. Sorry. I'm just a bit excited. Go on.'

He drew a sharp breath and his lean, handsome face grew grave. She tensed, realising he was about to state some uncomfortable things. 'When we…when I… Look, I realised when I got on the plane—no, even before I was on the plane—that I was—walking away from my life.' He closed his eyes for an instant, as if in remembered anguish. 'My—love. I knew I was—hurting you. But I felt…' He tightened his grip on her hands. His dark eyes held a sincere, earnest light that made her heart tremble. 'I was in black despair. I felt you deserved better than me. You *do* deserve better. But, the truth is, I couldn't bear—*can't* bear—being without you. The further away from you I went, the more I needed to be with you. These last few weeks, I've been in hell. I hope you can forgive me for being such a bastard. And a fool.' The ardent glow in his eyes intensified. 'I love you, Sophy.'

'Oh.' Her eyes filled with tears. 'Oh, darling, I love you. You must know I love you.'

'Thank God.' He kissed her and held her so close, she could feel his big, powerful heart thumping against hers. 'You know, when I was flying back, I wondered if I still had a chance with you.'

'Oh,' she breathed into his neck. 'Now you *are* being an idiot. Anyway, you aren't all that bad. You are quite kind, when you aren't mocking people. And you do rescue damsels in distress.'

'Only if they're especially hot.' He gazed down at her, smiling, then a faintly guilty tremor crossed his face. 'There are some things I've done I'm not proud of.'

'Maybe we both have.'

Connor looked quite taken aback for a second, but she didn't give him the chance to enquire what she meant. She put her arms around him and kissed him. It began as a gentle, loving kiss, but somehow fireworks ignited and threatened to waylay any further conversation.

Fortunately Connor broke the kiss when the cockpit was so steamed up it was impossible to see through the glass, and held her firmly away from him. 'Before we do anything else, there's something I need to know. You don't really mind that house up there on the Point, do you?'

She laughed. *Mind* it? 'Not really, no.'

'If we were to buy a bit of furniture, fix it up, purchase a few paintings and make it like a *home*, what do you think? Could you bear to live with me there and be my love?'

She nodded, her heart aglow with joy. 'I think I could.'

'So.' His dark eyes smiled into hers, and she knew what he was going to ask next. She could feel it in her bones. She had reached a truly fabulous seminal moment.

'Well, then, Sophy Woodruff, will you marry me?'

Her heart overflowed with happiness and love. 'Oh, Connor, *yes*.' She showered him with kisses. 'A *million times yes*.'

After some time, thinking about that house on the Point, and the work that needed to be done in the garden, she interrupted Connor's passionate appreciation of her to pant, 'You know, Connor, I have a very strong feeling—'

'Good,' he growled, his eyes burning with a fiery hunger. 'Because *I* have a very strong feeling.'

All night long, the boat rocked on the bosom of the waves.

ROMANCE

Untamed Billionaire, Undressed Virgin	Anna Cleary
Pleasure, Pregnancy and a Proposition	Heidi Rice
Exposed: Misbehaving with the Magnate	Kelly Hunter
Pregnant by the Playboy Tycoon	Anne Oliver
The Secret Mistress Arrangement	Kimberly Lang
The Marcolini Blackmail Marriage	Melanie Milburne
Bought: One Night, One Marriage	Natalie Anderson
Confessions of a Millionaire's Mistress	Robyn Grady
Housekeeper at His Beck and Call	Susan Stephens
Public Scandal, Private Mistress	Susan Napier
Surrender to the Playboy Sheikh	Kate Hardy
The Magnate's Indecent Proposal	Ally Blake
His Mistress, His Terms	Trish Wylie
The Boss's Bedroom Agenda	Nicola Marsh
Master of Mallarinka & Hired: His Personal Assistant	Way & Steele
The Lucchesi Bride & Adopted: One Baby	Winters & Oakley
An Italian Affair	Margaret McDonagh
Small Miracles	Jennifer Taylor

HISTORICAL

One Unashamed Night	Sophia James
The Captain's Mysterious Lady	Mary Nichols
The Major and the Pickpocket	Lucy Ashford

MEDICAL™

A Winter Bride	Meredith Webber
A Dedicated Lady	Gill Sanderson
An Unexpected Choice	Alison Roberts
Nice And Easy	Josie Metcalfe

1209 Gen Std LP

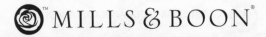

JANUARY 2010 LARGE PRINT TITLES

ROMANCE

Marchese's Forgotten Bride	Michelle Reid
The Brazilian Millionaire's Love-Child	Anne Mather
Powerful Greek, Unworldly Wife	Sarah Morgan
The Virgin Secretary's Impossible Boss	Carole Mortimer
Claimed: Secret Royal Son	Marion Lennox
Expecting Miracle Twins	Barbara Hannay
A Trip with the Tycoon	Nicola Marsh
Invitation to the Boss's Ball	Fiona Harper

HISTORICAL

The Piratical Miss Ravenhurst	Louise Allen
His Forbidden Liaison	Joanna Maitland
An Innocent Debutante in Hanover Square	Anne Herries

MEDICAL™

The Valtieri Marriage Deal	Caroline Anderson
The Rebel and the Baby Doctor	Joanna Neil
The Country Doctor's Daughter	Gill Sanderson
Surgeon Boss, Bachelor Dad	Lucy Clark
The Greek Doctor's Proposal	Molly Evans
Single Father: Wife and Mother Wanted	Sharon Archer

0110 Gen Std HB

MILLS & BOON

FEBRUARY 2010 HARDBACK TITLES

ROMANCE

At the Boss's Beck and Call	Anna Cleary
Hot-Shot Tycoon, Indecent Proposal	Heidi Rice
Revealed: A Prince and A Pregnancy	Kelly Hunter
Hot Boss, Wicked Nights	Anne Oliver
The Millionaire's Misbehaving Mistress	Kimberly Lang
Between the Italian's Sheets	Natalie Anderson
Naughty Nights in the Millionaire's Mansion	Robyn Grady
Sheikh Boss, Hot Desert Nights	Susan Stephens
Bought: One Damsel in Distress	Lucy King
The Billionaire's Bought Mistress	Annie West
Playboy Boss, Pregnancy of Passion	Kate Hardy
A Night with the Society Playboy	Ally Blake
One Night with the Rebel Billionaire	Trish Wylie
Two Weeks in the Magnate's Bed	Nicola Marsh
Magnate's Mistress…Accidentally Pregnant	Kimberly Lang
Desert Prince, Blackmailed Bride	Kim Lawrence
The Nurse's Baby Miracle	Janice Lynn
Second Lover	Gill Sanderson

HISTORICAL

The Rake and the Heiress	Marguerite Kaye
Wicked Captain, Wayward Wife	Sarah Mallory
The Pirate's Willing Captive	Anne Herries

MEDICAL

Angel's Christmas	Caroline Anderson
Someone To Trust	Jennifer Taylor
Morrison's Magic	Abigail Gordon
Wedding Bells	Meredith Webber

FEBRUARY 2010 LARGE PRINT TITLES

ROMANCE

Desert Prince, Bride of Innocence	Lynne Graham
Raffaele: Taming His Tempestuous Virgin	Sandra Marton
The Italian Billionaire's Secretary Mistress	Sharon Kendrick
Bride, Bought and Paid For	Helen Bianchin
Betrothed: To the People's Prince	Marion Lennox
The Bridesmaid's Baby	Barbara Hannay
The Greek's Long-Lost Son	Rebecca Winters
His Housekeeper Bride	Melissa James

HISTORICAL

The Brigadier's Daughter	Catherine March
The Wicked Baron	Sarah Mallory
His Runaway Maiden	June Francis

MEDICAL™

Emergency: Wife Lost and Found	Carol Marinelli
A Special Kind of Family	Marion Lennox
Hot-Shot Surgeon, Cinderella Bride	Alison Roberts
A Summer Wedding at Willowmere	Abigail Gordon
Miracle: Twin Babies	Fiona Lowe
The Playboy Doctor Claims His Bride	Janice Lynn

millsandboon.co.uk Community

Join Us!

The Community is the perfect place to meet and chat to kindred spirits who love books and reading as much as you do, but it's also the place to:

- **Get the inside scoop from authors about their latest books**
- **Learn how to write a romance book with advice from our editors**
- **Help us to continue publishing the best in women's fiction**
- **Share your thoughts on the books we publish**
- **Befriend other users**

Forums: Interact with each other as well as authors, editors and a whole host of other users worldwide.

Blogs: Every registered community member has their own blog to tell the world what they're up to and what's on their mind.

Book Challenge: We're aiming to read 5,000 books and have joined forces with The Reading Agency in our inaugural Book Challenge.

Profile Page: Showcase yourself and keep a record of your recent community activity.

Social Networking: We've added buttons at the end of every post to share via digg, Facebook, Google, Yahoo, technorati and de.licio.us.

www.millsandboon.co.uk